W9-BYJ-847

PRISONER
OF WAR

ALSO BY MICHAEL P. SPRADLIN

The Enemy Above

Into the Killing Seas

The Killer Species series:

Menace from the Deep

Feeding Frenzy

Out for Blood

Ultimate Attack

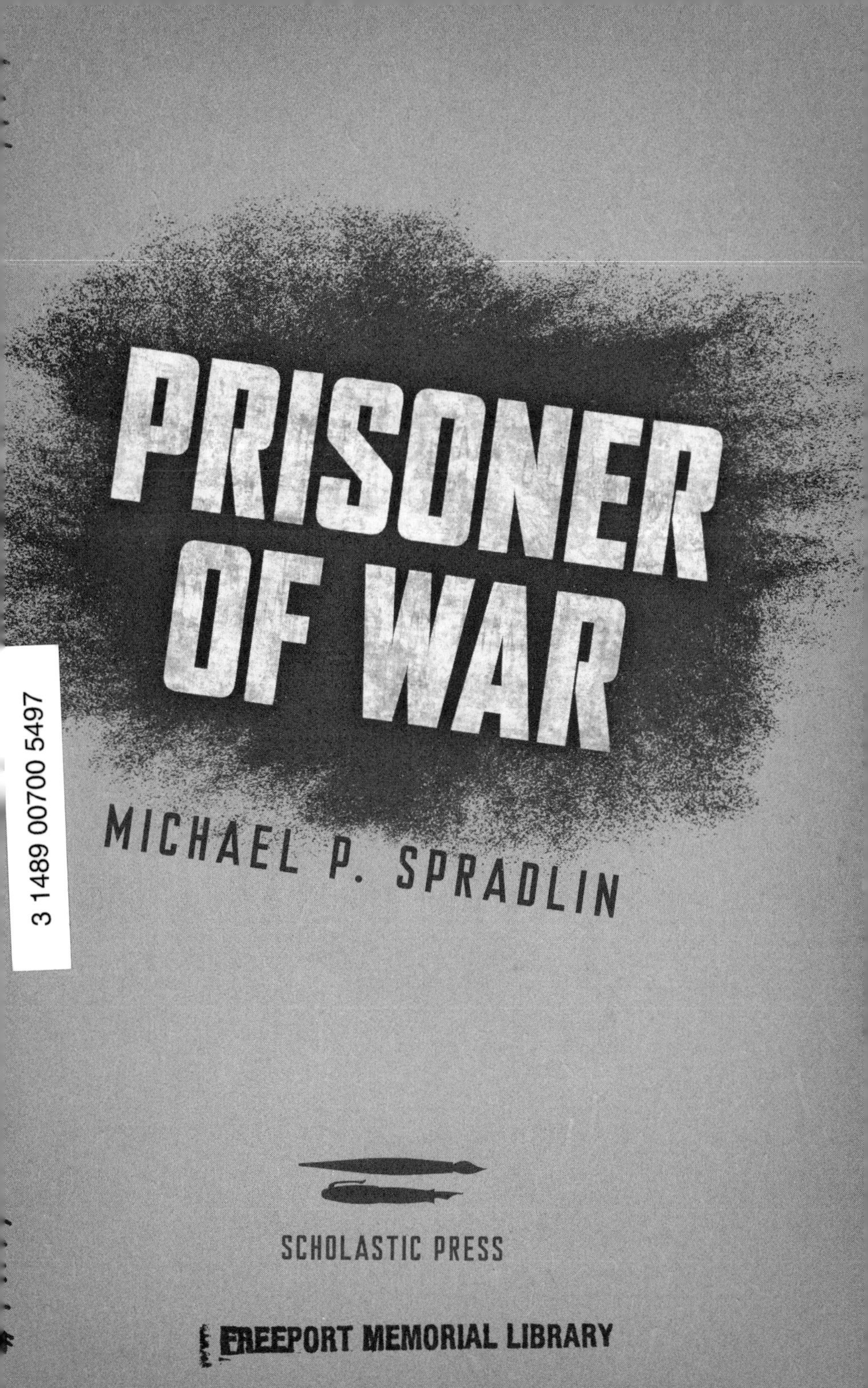

PRISONER OF WAR

MICHAEL P. SPRADLIN

SCHOLASTIC PRESS

Library of Congress Cataloging-in-Publication Data

Names: Spradlin, Michael P., author.
Title: Prisoner of war / Michael P. Spradlin.
Description: First edition. | New York : Scholastic Press, 2017. | Summary: Fifteen-year-old Henry Forrest lies about his age and enlists in the Marines to escape from his abusive father, but when he is immediately sent to the Philippines he finds himself in the middle of the Japanese invasion—and as he grows up he will have to endure the Bataan Death March, overcrowded prisons, and the Japanese factory in Tokyo where he is eventually sent as slave labor.
Identifiers: LCCN 2016040575 | ISBN 9780545857833
Subjects: LCSH: World War, 1939–1945—Prisoners and prisons, Japanese—Juvenile fiction. | Bataan Death March, Philippines, 1942—Juvenile fiction. | Forced labor—Japan—Juvenile fiction. | Survival—Juvenile fiction. | Philippines—History—Japanese occupation, 1942–1945—Juvenile fiction. | Tokyo (Japan)—History—Bombardment, 1944–1945—Juvenile fiction. | CYAC: World War, 1939–1945—Prisoners and prisons, Japanese—Fiction. | Bataan Death March, Philippines, 1942—Fiction. | Forced labor—Fiction. | Survival—Fiction. | Philippines—History—Japanese occupation, 1942–1945—Fiction. | Tokyo (Japan)—History—Bombardment, 1944–1945—Fiction. | Japan—History—1926–1945—Fiction.
Classification: LCC PZ7.S7645 Pr 2017 | DDC 813.54 [Fic] —dc23
LC record available at https://lccn.loc.gov/2016040575

10 9 8 7 6 5 4 3 2 1 17 18 19 20 21

Printed in the U.S.A. 23

First edition, July 2017

Book design by Christopher Stengel

This book is lovingly dedicated to all the men and women of the Allied forces who endured their imprisonment in a Japanese POW camp with courage and honor. The free world owes each one of you a debt it can never repay.

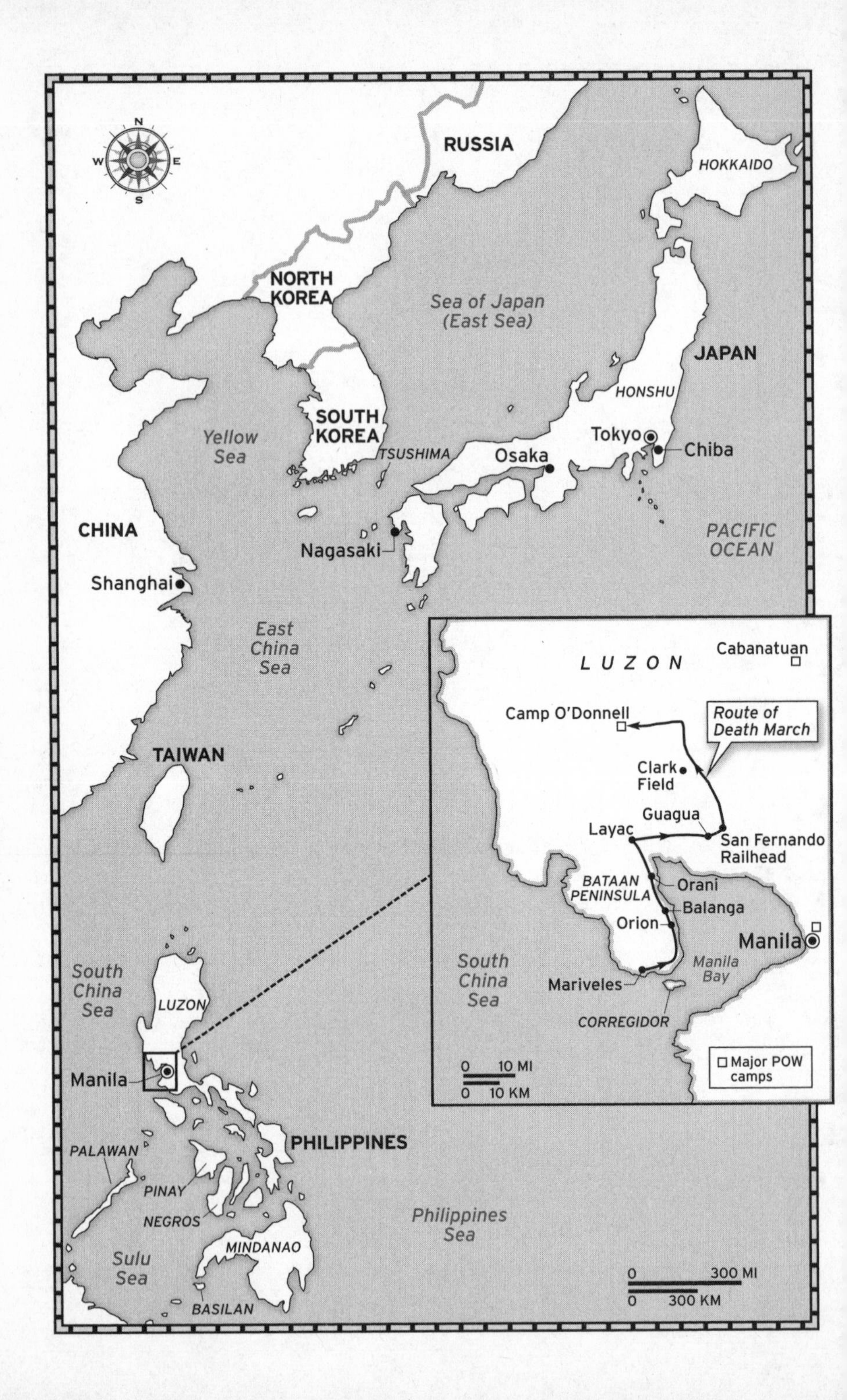

N
W
E
S
RUSSIA
HOKKAIDO
NORTH KOREA
Sea of Japan (East Sea)
JAPAN
HONSHU
SOUTH KOREA
Yellow Sea
Tokyo
Chiba
TSUSHIMA
Osaka
CHINA
Nagasaki
PACIFIC OCEAN
Shanghai
East China Sea
TAIWAN
South China Sea
LUZON
Manila
PHILIPPINES
PALAWAN
PINAY
NEGROS
MINDANAO
Sulu Sea
BASILAN
Philippines Sea
0 300 MI
0 300 KM
LUZON
Cabanatuan
Camp O'Donnell
Route of Death March
Clark Field
Guagua
Layac
San Fernando Railhead
BATAAN PENINSULA
Orani
Balanga
Orion
Manila
South China Sea
Manila Bay
Mariveles
CORREGIDOR
0 10 MI
0 10 KM
Major POW camps

The history of free men is never really written by chance, but by choice: their choice!

—Dwight D. Eisenhower

PROLOGUE

When my mom died, my home became a war zone. And my father was the enemy. Surly and resentful, he took out his anger on me. It's ironic that to escape one war, I ran away and found another. But it wasn't a war I chose. It was chosen for me.

She died when I was seven, and I spent every day of the next eight years of my life terrified of my father. That isn't how it's supposed to be. A kid shouldn't be afraid of a parent. I might have been young, but even then I knew that much. I don't know why he blamed me for my mother's death, but he did. She died in a car accident. I was at school. If I'd been in the backseat distracting her—begging her to stop for an ice-cream cone the way I always did—maybe I'd understand why my pa was angry. My grandpa tried to convince me that it wasn't my fault. That my dad was just so heartbroken he needed to blame someone for his loss. Pa chose me.

Six months after she died, when the shock finally wore off, things got really bad. My father always had a temper. But after the accident, Pa was angry all the time. I couldn't do anything right. I'd clean up the supper table, and if I made too much noise putting the dishes in the sink, I'd get a backhanded slap across the cheek.

"Stop making so much dang noise!" he'd shout.

If I missed a speck of dirt sweeping the kitchen, he'd go berserk and chase me around the house with a wooden spoon.

"What are you, blind? Can't even sweep a floor! You're good for nothin'! Nothin'!"

We lived on a farm, and I had to do most of the chores. Milk the cows, feed the hogs and chickens before school, and in the spring, I'd even have to plow and plant. He worked me pretty hard. But I didn't mind the work. I actually liked farming. I loved the feel of the soil in my hands. The crunch of the late fall frost under my feet as I walked from the house to the barn. And doing all those chores gave me a few moments every day when I didn't have to be afraid. Hogs and chickens never yell at you.

Our farm was a beautiful spot—eighty acres on a rolling hillside outside of Duluth. My mother had loved it. I remember her working in her garden and feeding the animals in the morning. She would sing while she did it. She was barely over five feet tall, but farm life had made her strong. Somehow Pa stayed in line when she was alive. She made him happy. I could never quite figure out how she did it. But when she died, a piece of him did, too.

Nothing I did ever pleased him. And when he started drinking, things got even worse. He'd go into town after I got home from school. I'd be doing my homework after finishing my chores, and when he came home he'd always find something to pick at me about.

He started with the belt when I was nine. That was the worst.

It's a horrible thing to live your life in fear. My grandpa would try to get him to leave me alone. But Grandpa was my mother's father, a small, quiet man who'd lived on the farm since before I was born. He'd emigrated from Norway, and what English he spoke came out with a thick accent. Pa would just belittle him.

"What'd you say, old man? Get the marbles outta your mouth," he'd grouse.

I don't know why Grandpa didn't leave. But I guess, like me, he had no place else to go. Maybe he stayed for me. To give whatever comfort he could. Or because this was where his daughter had lived. Whenever Grandpa said anything about the way Pa was treating me, my father would come down extra hard on me. "Blast it, Henry! I swear, I might as well go find me a four-year-old girl to come and do your chores for you. Maybe then they'd get done right."

"Yes, Pa. Sorry," I'd mutter. And try to make myself scarce.

No matter what I did, it was never enough. When I was ten I quit going to school. I was tired of explaining the black eyes and the welts on my cheeks. Mrs. King, my fourth-grade teacher, would quiz me about my bruises and cuts.

"Henry, what happened?" she would ask.

I'd always make something up, worried that if I said anything, it would just get worse. Mrs. King was persistent.

"Henry, are you sure you're all right?" She was a nice lady. Her face was round and her eyes sparkled with kindness. She had curly black hair and wore glasses. In some ways she reminded me of my mother. I hated lying to her, but by then I was so scared of Pa that I couldn't say anything except, "Yes, ma'am, just an accident. My grandpa says I'm just at that clumsy age. And last week one of the roosters took after me and pecked my face good. I don't like that old rooster."

It hadn't always been like this. When my mother was alive, Pa was different. He would still get angry and surly, but she had a way of calming everyone she met. She would smile and look at you—really look at you—and it just made everything seem fine. I had a picture of her in my room. After she died, I found that when I wasn't in the room staring at her picture, it was getting harder and harder to remember her face. There was so much turmoil in the house it was like she stood at the far end of some long hallway of my memory. And every day her presence faded from what had once been a happy home.

"Your mother was too soft on you," Pa would yell when he was in one of his tempers. "She turned you into a weakling." I tried as hard as I could not to act afraid and I never cried in front of him, no matter what he did. No matter how scared I was.

I used to pray that he would come home drunk and pass out so he would leave me alone. When I turned fourteen that was usually what happened. Grandpa and I had to work like demons to keep the farm running. And while all this was happening, I was growing. Farm work was making me strong. When I was fifteen, I was six feet, three inches tall. Almost as big as my dad.

Most people would say, "You're strong now, Henry. Stand up to him. You don't have to take it anymore." Most people would be wrong. I might have been nearly as big and strong as he was, but I didn't have anywhere near his anger or fury in my heart. If I'd done that, I knew I'd be letting my mother down. I'd be more like him than her.

Getting away from him was my only chance. If I didn't, nothing would ever change. He would continue hating me, and I would never stop being afraid. Right after my fifteenth birthday, the answer came to me. I would run away and join the Marines.

It turned out to be remarkably easy. First I told my grandpa what I was going to do. I needed his help. Without it, I'd be stuck under Pa's thumb forever.

"No, Henry, no," he pleaded.

"Grandpa, I'm sorry. But I can't stay here anymore. And I can't get away unless you help me."

Finally he agreed. The next day, while Pa was off doing who knows what, we drove into Duluth. There was a United States Marine Corps recruiting station right on Main Street. Grandpa parked the truck, and we made our way into the office.

A tall man in a green uniform sat behind a desk. His face was all sharp angles, and his hair was trimmed in a crew cut. His uniform didn't have a piece of lint or anything out of place on it. There were three stripes on his sleeve.

"Help you?" he asked.

"Yes, sir," I said. "I'm here to enlist."

"First, it's not sir, it's Sergeant. And second, how old are you?"

Grandpa stood next to me clutching his felt hat in both hands. I knew he was nervous. I hoped he wouldn't give it away.

"I'm eighteen, si—Sergeant. Born October 11, 1923."

"You got a birth certificate? Something proves that?"

"No, Sergeant. I don't. I checked at the courthouse and I guess my ma and pa never got around to filing one."

"I need proof of your age," he said.

"Well, I heard if you had a relative who could confirm your age, you could join up. My grandpa is here. He can vouch for me."

The sergeant looked at me, his eyes narrowing. Then he shifted his gaze to Grandpa. He studied him, and I could see Gramps starting to wilt. I had to get this over with quick.

"Grandpa, can you tell the sergeant? My birthday is October 11, 1923. Isn't that right?"

"Yah," he said, nodding. "Yah." Whenever Grandpa got nervous or stressed his Norwegian accent got thicker.

"He doesn't speak a whole lot of English," I said.

"Is that right?" the sergeant said. His face was a mask of stone. I could not tell what he was thinking. He turned his gaze from Grandpa back to me. I could see Grandpa relax from the corner of my eye.

"What's your name, boy?" he asked.

"Henry Forrest."

"Why do you want to join the Marines?"

"Well . . . Sergeant, I always heard the Marines was the finest fighting force there is. And that's what I want to be. I want to be one of the finest."

I could tell I'd struck a nerve with the sergeant. The corners of his lips lifted up in a smile, just for the briefest of moments.

"You know it ain't going to be easy," he said.

"Yes, Sergeant, I know. But I've wanted to be a Marine since I was a kid."

He wasn't quite convinced.

"Where are your parents?"

"My ma died when I was seven. My pa ran off a couple years ago. Grandpa raised me mostly."

The sergeant steepled his fingers and stared at me. I was afraid it wasn't going to work. If it didn't I'd try the Army or the Navy.

He sat up straight and opened a desk drawer.

"You need to fill out some forms," he said. He slid a few pages across his desk and handed me a pen. I filled them out as fast as I could and signed my name, pushing them back to him.

"Congratulations. You're on your way to being a Marine. And you're in luck. There's a train tomorrow leaving for Parris Island. That's where you'll do your basic training." He pulled out another small booklet and filled it out, then tore out a strip of paper. "This is your ticket," he said, handing it to me. "Don't miss the train."

I didn't miss the train. But after all that came next, I would come to wish I had.

PART ONE

INVASION

December 8, 1941

CHAPTER ONE

DISCOVERED

I stood firmly at attention. The only sound in the office was the whirring of the ceiling fan. All it succeeded in doing was pushing the hot and humid air around the room. Colonel William Forsythe sat at his desk, the top of which was empty except for a single file. I'd known it was my personnel file even if I hadn't seen my photograph clipped to it. Why else would I be here, a lowly private ordered to report to the colonel's office?

The old man was dressed in the usual khaki uniform. His tie was neatly knotted and lay straight on his shirt, and I wondered how he could stand it in this weather. There were never any sweat stains under the old man's arms or around his collar. I had no idea how he did it. I could feel perspiration on my neck, flooding down my back. I imagined my shirt was drenched.

"Did you think we wouldn't find out?" the colonel asked.

"I don't understand, sir," I barked in reply.

The colonel leaned back in his chair and stared at me. His face was tanned and lined from the sun. His crew cut showed snow-white hair all around his skull. He took a deep breath and puffed out his cheeks, letting the air out slowly.

"It's over, boy," the colonel said. "You're underage. I don't know how you got into the Marines, but I know how you are going to get out. You'll return to the barracks to pack up your gear. You know, before I joined the Corps, I was in the cavalry." He droned on, but Henry wasn't paying attention. Something about how "things were different then, and the military didn't tolerate the kind of shenanigans Henry was trying to pull."

The colonel leaned back in his chair and put his feet up on his desk. He was wearing leather riding boots. They were shined to a high gloss and reached all the way to his knees. Colonel Forsythe had been in the Marines almost forty years. He served in the cavalry and chased Pancho Villa with General Black Jack Pershing on the US-Mexico border. He'd served in World War I and was as old school as it came regarding rules and regulations. Pretty much everyone in the regiment hated him. Some of the sergeants had some pretty salty names for him. The nicest one was Colonel Fourhours. They said that was how long it took him to tell one of his war stories.

"Colonel Forsythe, sir," I said. "There must be some mistake, sir!"

"Knock it off, Private," the colonel said. "It's over. I admire your chutzpah, but you're fifteen years old. How long did you think you were going to get away with it?"

The office was quiet, except for the clicking sound of the fan. The truth of it was, I hated being stationed here in the Philippines. I'd had no idea where I'd be sent when I joined the Marines. I had hoped it would be Europe. Instead I'd been sent to this miserable jungle. The weather was always hot and damp. It rained a lot. There was never a breeze in the barracks. It was awful.

I had no skills when I joined up. Bailing hay and plowing fields didn't translate to much that the Marines needed. Turns out they didn't grow a lot of hay in the United States Marine Corps, so I ended up in the infantry. I thought enlisting would be like joining a fraternity. That between drills, me and the other marines would pull pranks on each other and talk about the movie starlets who starred in our dreams. But I barely got through basic training. It was grueling, and it took everything I had to push through. Then when I arrived in the Philippines to begin my tour, it turned out to be just like basic training only hotter. I marched and fired my rifle on the range. My platoon practiced close order drill in the heat until I thought I would drop. I'd thought basic would kill me. What a fool I'd been. But as wrong as I'd been about enlisting, I still wanted to stay.

The trouble was, the colonel had me dead to rights. I stood at attention wondering if everything I had concocted was about to come apart. This couldn't happen. If they sent me back, I'd have nowhere to go. I had to find a way to convince the colonel and the Marines that I was legal.

But I wasn't sure how I'd do it. While the colonel glared at me, I considered my options. If I told anyone in my company what was happening, I'd be admitting guilt. Not only that, I could get them in trouble, too. I wanted to rush back to the barracks and find the two men I'd become closest to: my platoon leader, Gunnery Sergeant Jack McAdams, and my best bud, Billy Jamison. They would tell me what to do. Gunny would get me out of this mess. Ever since I'd been assigned to his squad he'd watched out for me. I wished he were here now. But he wasn't. I had to face the colonel alone.

"Pack your gear," Colonel Forsythe ordered. "You're on a plane to Guam tomorrow, and from there to Pearl Harbor. What they do with you when you get there ain't my problem—"

The colonel's words were cut short as the ground beneath us trembled. At first, I thought an earthquake had rent the earth. The office shook hard, throwing the colonel to the floor. I was nearly knocked off my feet and had to grab the desk to keep from tumbling to the ground. The sound of a massive explosion was so loud I thought my eardrums had burst. This was no earthquake. We were being bombed.

I hustled around the desk and helped the colonel to his feet. Another explosion rocked the office, and this time we both lurched to the ground. Overhead, I heard the buzzing of planes. For weeks, there had been rumors that the Japanese were going to attack. Could it be?

I helped the colonel stand up once again. The old man was disheveled and covered in dust. There was nothing neat about his uniform now.

"Orders, sir?"

The colonel raced to the office window and peered out at the sky above. "Get down!" he shouted.

Another bomb whistled overhead. I thought for sure that it would kill us. We hit the floor and covered our heads. But it kept going and exploded several hundred yards away.

The colonel staggered to his feet. His eyes were wild and his hands shook. It was pretty clear he had no idea what to do. *This is the Marines for you*, I thought. *They give us a CO who doesn't have a clue.*

"Orders, sir?" I asked again.

"Uh . . . you . . . report to your unit, Marine. Yes . . . report to your unit."

I saluted. "Yes, sir!"

I ran to the office door, gazing out to make sure the sky was clear. Seeing no planes, I ran toward the barracks. My secret may have been found out, and maybe they'd be sending me home. But for now, at least, I was still a rifleman in the United States Marine Corps.

And there was fighting to do.

CHAPTER TWO

BESIEGED

I had a big head. It had been a real trial for the quartermaster to find me a helmet. I had to remove the liner on the one he'd given me, and it still fit me like a second skin. Sweat poured down my head and face and soaked the T-shirt beneath my blouse. I pulled off the blouse, unable to stand wearing it in the heat. But if I was being honest with myself, I was sweating as much from nerves as I was from the temperature.

For the last month, the Japanese had bombed the Philippines nearly nonstop. Our military forces were unprepared and overmatched. The Japanese were hitting American bases all over the South Pacific. The worst attack had been at Pearl Harbor in Hawaii. Reports over the radio said that several battleships had been destroyed and thousands of men killed and injured.

But as much as I worried for my brothers-in-arms at Pearl Harbor, I was terrified about what would happen to my own company. We were stationed on Luzon, the largest island of the Philippines. We'd been based near Manila, the capital city, but when the Japanese began bombing, we evacuated to the southern peninsula of Bataan. It kept the Japanese from hitting us overland, the terrain was rough, and we could bottle them up and inflict heavy casualties if we needed to. But in the end it didn't matter—the Japanese forces set their sights on us. They destroyed most of the American planes at the Bataan airfield before our boys even had a chance to get airborne.

Once, at the airfield, I watched as Japanese pilots shot their machine guns along the fuselage of a plane parked on the ground. Then they would turn a tight figure eight in the sky and come about and stitch bullets along the wings, completely destroying the aircraft. They reminded me of dragonflies darting about.

Without even thinking, I removed the clip from my rifle and inspected it. I snapped it back into place and raised the gun to my eye, sighting down the barrel.

"I think it's in workin' order, Tree," Gunnery Sergeant McAdams said. Gunny had called me Tree since I'd first been assigned to his unit. He'd stood in the barracks in an undershirt and his fatigues, chewing half a cigar in the corner of his mouth. Snatching my orders out of my hand, he'd studied them. "Forrest, Henry. No middle initial, huh?" he'd said. "Well, yer for darn sure as big as a tree, I'll give you that. Pick a bunk and stow yer gear." After that, the nickname Tree had stuck. I didn't mind. My dad called me plenty worse names.

"You just make sure you're savin' them bullets for the Japanese, Tree," my friend Jamison said. Where Gunny was wide and solid, Corporal Billy Jamison was tall and thin. He was deceptively strong and quick, as I'd learned in our hand-to-hand combat training exercises when I'd first arrived in the Philippines. He was wiry and had a certain kind of twitchy nervousness about him I found disconcerting. But he looked out for me. He kept the bullies and the tough guys in the battalion off my back. He often told me, "Kid, you got the makings of a squared away Marine. But I'll tell you true. You're gonna have to get a whole lot meaner and a whole lot tougher if you're gonna make it in the Corps. You're strong as an ox and you got a brain on your shoulders. That's a good combination. Me and Gunny is gonna train you up, but you already got a head start on most of the jamokes in this outfit. Just don't be afraid to use that brain of yours." Except for Grandpa, I never had anyone treat me like Gunny and Jamison. Like they respected me. Sure they teased me and poked fun at my "baby face," as Gunny called it. Sometimes I was awkward and clumsy when we'd practice close order drill.

And Jamison would laugh and say, "Boy, you are such a gink." But they accepted me. They treated me like a man.

Now the three of us sat huddled in a machine gun emplacement, behind sandbags filled with several hundred pounds of dirt. We were positioned on the west side of the southern end of the island. Command had determined that if the Japanese sent ground troops, they would land here. We were dug in on a small rise about two hundred yards from the beach, waiting.

When the Japanese arrived, Gunny would be operating the .50 caliber machine gun. Jamison would load the gun and cool the barrel when it grew too hot to fire. My job would be to lay down suppressing fire whenever they stopped shooting to reload. We had a dozen metal boxes of ammunition for the .50 cal, and I hoped it would be enough. Each box held about three hundred rounds. It took Jamison about fifteen seconds to reload. With eight shots in my clip, I would have to be accurate. Ammunition was in short supply, and there were not a lot of .50 caliber machine guns in the Philippines. The gun was too big and heavy for jungle fighting. But the higher-ups had scrounged up the remaining ones they could find and had them brought here on a flatbed truck.

"When do you think the Japanese will get here?" I asked.

"About five minutes sooner'n the last time ya asked," Gunny said.

"Sorry, Gunny. Just nervous," I said.

"You'd best try and relax, Tree," Jamison said. "Old Man Forsythe says reinforcements are on the way. None of our aircraft carriers were in port when they hit Pearl. They're all headin' here with plenty of planes. There's even more of 'em flyin' up from Australia. We'll have our air support back. Then we'll see how the Japanese Imperial flyboys like zoomin' around when there's somebody shootin' back."

Jamison and Gunny were seasoned Marines. Gunny had been in the Corps almost ten years, and Jams was in the second year of a four-year hitch. From the moment I arrived, I was struck by the feeling both of them knew instinctively how young I was and had made it their business to see I got trained up right.

I hadn't had much time to think about what had happened in the colonel's office. It seemed like such a long time ago. No one had said anything to me since. With the Japanese about to invade, I guess I had moved way down on the priority list. I had a feeling Gunny and Jams knew Forsythe was about to ship me out. They hadn't said anything. But it felt like they had been paying special attention to me once the bombs started falling. When the reinforcements arrived and the Japanese were beaten back, I was going home. I had no idea what would happen when I got there. Would the Marines discharge me or would they send me to jail? It was hard not to think about.

"This whole thing don't make sense," Gunny said. "If reinforcements are comin', where in heck are they? We're waitin' here, on this miserable, wide spot in the ocean, lined up like sittin' ducks. I'd feel a whole lot better if this so-called peninsula was separated from the main island."

Jamison and I were quiet. Gunny was a smart non-commissioned officer and knew his onions when it came to strategy and tactics. Most of the enlisted men didn't believe anyone was coming to reinforce us. It had been a month since the Japanese had invaded the Philippines. They controlled the skies, and like Gunny said, they had done more than a fair job of destroying just about every military asset on the islands.

Now that the Japanese held most of Luzon, including its airfield and the capital city of Manila, they had set their sights on Bataan. And even though some of our troops had managed to retreat to our present location, we were still outgunned and outmanned. Right now, the emperor's military controlled most of the South Pacific. Gunny knew we were in trouble, and he studied his map every night, marking it up with a pencil.

"Our boys is all the way down here," he'd say, pointing to the Solomon Islands, far south of the Philippines and closer to Australia. "They could practically throw rocks and hit the Aussies, who ain't in any better shape than we are. I think them reinforcements ain't comin' here until they secure Australia. If Yamamoto gets that far, we might as well hang 'er up." Yamamoto was the commander of the Imperial Japanese Navy, and after the sneak attack on Pearl Harbor, he had become enemy number one to everyone in the US military.

We kept watch on the horizon, studying the ocean, looking for any sign of ships or planes. The waiting was becoming unbearable. Part of me wished the attack would just come, and then we could get it over with. We might lose. But win or lose, the endless, nerve-wracking waiting would cease.

I scanned the beach. There were more machine gun emplacements to our left and right extending along the rise. Behind us, in the tree line, were tanks and some howitzers, a few antiaircraft guns—whatever our remaining forces had been able to scrounge up. The tanks were camouflaged with netting and foliage to disguise them from the Japanese. But whenever they opened fire on incoming aircraft they had to move the guns and tanks to a new location so the enemy planes couldn't target them on their next attack.

This morning, though, all was quiet. The skies were clear. While we appreciated the silence, it only served to make everyone edgy. I swore I could hear each tick of the second hand on my watch. The tension was eating at me. The waves crashing on the beach sounded like cannon shots. The breeze off the ocean was hot and wet—it whistled in my ears like a typhoon. I wished I were back in the barracks napping. Except the barracks had been destroyed a week ago. I tried to focus on the job at hand, but it was hard to keep my mind from wandering.

The sound of Gunny racking the slide on his machine gun snapped me back into focus.

"Look alive, fellas," he said. "Here they come!"

I gazed out at the water. Where moments ago the ocean had been an empty, endless blue, now it was dotted with Japanese barges and landing craft. The sky filled with airplanes of all shapes and sizes. Bombers, fighters, and torpedo planes buzzed at the island like a terrifying horde of bees.

The battle was on.

CHAPTER THREE

HOLDING OUT

I was mesmerized as the Japanese vessels grew closer to the beach. Time seemed to slow down. It was as if I stood at the end of a long tunnel. The sound took forever to reach me. I knew their landing craft and airplane engines were roaring and the gunshots and bombs were exploding. But in my mind everything moved in soundless slow motion.

"Tree! Tree! Henry!" Gunny's gravelly voice finally broke through my trance. I swiveled my head around to look at him. "Look alive, Tree!" he shouted. "They come in another thousand yards and I'm lightin' up them boats, so be ready. Once the shootin' starts we're in line for a lot of attention, and it ain't gonna be the friendly kind. When Jamison changes out that ammo belt, look for targets shootin' at us and hit 'em back hard. Slow and steady. Remember what I told ya on the range. Aim small, miss small. Ya can do this, son!"

I nodded at him. I wanted to swallow, but my mouth was too dry. I couldn't tell Gunny how scared I was.

The truth of it was, I didn't believe I *could* do it. I knew how to use a gun. But I'd never done anything more than shoot on the range. Now I'd have to shoot at men, flesh and blood human beings. If I didn't, my friends could die. *How did I get myself into this?* I thought of home, my father and grandfather and how bad it was living there. But for the first time in my life, I wished I were there rather than here.

The first wave of airplanes reached the shore. Their machine guns riddled the beach, and sand flew everywhere. I could see the bomb bay doors open on the attack bombers as they released their payloads like huge metal chickens laying eggs. A few seconds later the explosions shook the ground, and the planes pulled up, disappearing behind us. As the landing craft drew nearer, I watched the helmeted heads of the Japanese soldiers as they bobbed in the waves.

When Gunny opened fire with the .50 cal, the noise made me jump. The bullets carved their way across the sand and splashed into the water until Gunny adjusted the range. The machine gun rounds ripped into the Japanese landing barges, punching large holes in their thin metal sides. The barges took on water, forcing the men aboard over the side and into the waves.

Still they came.

When the first Japanese barge hit the beach, Gunny cut down the entire boat. Not a man was left standing. But now our position was drawing fire from the Japanese gunners above.

"Get down!" Jamison shouted. Bullets whizzed and plunked into the sandbags around us. We ducked beneath the top of the emplacement. When there was a pause in the shooting, Gunny opened up again. The magazine on the gun clanged as the belt emptied.

"Now! Now!" he shouted. "Go, Tree! Suppressin' fire!"

I laid my rifle on a sandbag and sighted down the barrel, looking for targets. There were Japanese soldiers all over the beach. I tried to focus, but when I pulled the trigger I was pretty sure I missed. I kept shooting until the empty clip ejected from my rifle with a metallic ringing sound.

Pulling another from my ammo belt, I tapped the pointed shells on my helmet and snapped the clip into place. I racked a round into the chamber and took aim. I had never been so scared in my life.

The .50 cal barked again. Hundreds of rounds rained down on the Japanese soldiers. Gunny had a steady aim, and with each burst of the gun, men spun screaming into the sand. It felt like hours had passed. I lost count of how many times we changed out the belt on the machine gun. Empty clips from my rifle littered the ground. I don't know how many times I fired my weapon. Finally, the landing barges stopped coming and the planes disappeared from the sky. All was quiet.

"They was just probin'," Gunny said. "Tryin' to get a sense of our defenses. They'll be back, and there'll be a lot more of 'em."

"What do we do?" I asked, watching as Gunny reached into his blouse pocket for the half a cigar he carried around with him. He lit it and took three puffs before rubbing it out. Like everything else, there was a shortage of cigars, and he was trying to make this one last.

Returning it to his pocket, Gunny shrugged. "I reckon we fight."

I tried not to shudder. I didn't know if I could survive another attack. It wasn't even the idea of getting shot that bothered me. It was the not knowing. The confusion and chaos of battle made me feel all twisted up inside. Now I was bone tired. My shoulder ached from firing the rifle.

"When do you think they're comin' back, Gunny?" Jamison asked.

"I don't know," Gunny said. "But if it was me, I'd come at night. Make it a darn sight harder for us to spot 'em."

"What do we do?" I asked again. Too nervous to ask anything else.

"I don't know that, either, son," Gunny said. "But right now I reckon we better get to movin' this gun."

The defensive line along the ridge came alive with activity. Tanks rolled along the tree line taking up new positions. Groups of men were pulling the antiaircraft guns along the jungle floor. They would move everything. Undoubtedly, the Japanese planes had taken reconnaissance photos of the Americans' gun emplacements. When they came back, they wouldn't find their targets in the same place.

"We'll move fifty yards up the ridge. I'll break down the gun, y'all start movin' them sandbags," Gunny said. Gunny wasn't a tall man. In fact, I towered over him. But he was solid and strong, his shoulders wide and the muscles on his arms bulging out of his blouse like canned hams. He collapsed the tripod on the .50 cal and hoisted the gun over his shoulder.

"Let's move," he said.

Jams and I looked at each other. Neither of us relished the thought of lugging sandbags fifty yards away. On the other hand, the sandbags had kept us alive. We decided that on the whole it was worth doing. Jamison grabbed the end of one and I the other. After just a few steps we were breathing hard and sweating.

Gunny had found a spot with a natural depression in the sand. He was digging into the ground with an entrenching tool. We dropped the sandbag at the edge and trudged back for another. It took us an hour to move everything and get ready. A private from another unit came by with four more boxes of ammo for the .50 cal.

"How you set for ammo, Tree?" Gunny asked me.

I checked my ammo pouch and belt. "I got twelve clips left," I said.

"All right," Gunny said. "It'll be dark in a couple hours. Y'all stay here. Keep an eye on the sky. The planes'll come first. Get some chow. I'm gonna go try and scrounge up some more supplies."

We ate our rations and then I cleaned my rifle. As nighttime fell, Gunny still hadn't returned.

"Jams, can I ask you something?" I asked.

"Sure," Jamison said.

"Do you really think there are reinforcements coming?"

Jamison was quiet for a moment. He reached into his pocket for a cigarette and lit it. His silence made me uneasy.

"I gotta believe so, Tree. We may have lost a lot of battleships at Pearl Harbor. But there are carriers out there, and they all got a bunch of planes on 'em. They're headed this way. You can count on it."

A far-off buzzing sound drew our attention to the ocean. The noise grew closer. Both of us jumped in surprise when Gunny leapt into our new foxhole. He carried two boxes of ammo for the .50 cal and had a bandolier of M1 ammo around his chest.

"Get ready!" he shouted. "They's back!"

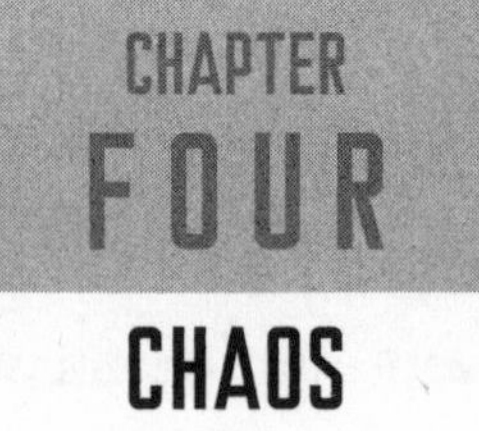

CHAPTER FOUR
CHAOS

The Japanese came back, and this time, as Gunny would say, "They wasn't messin' around." They had roughly double the number of troops from the first attack. The landing barges came in waves, and hundreds of soldiers piled onto the beach. From our position on the ridge, we laid down a withering fire.

This time we had built our sandbag wall higher, stacking them in such a way that the barrel of the machine gun poked through them rather than having to sit on top. This allowed Gunny to focus his field of fire, and it kept us safer below the top of the emplacement. We also built in a small port for me to use the rifle. When the first belt emptied I aimed through the rifle port and fired. There was so much confusion on the beach I couldn't tell if I hit anything. Japanese soldiers were falling like bowling pins.

The tanks and antiaircraft guns behind us thundered. One of them found its target as a Japanese Zero fighter plane exploded in the sky. I had to close my eyes to protect them from the fireball that lit up the night.

This attack was different from the last. The Japanese were gaining the advantage.

"We're gonna have to fall back!" Gunny shouted. "Jamison, cool that barrel!" Jamison grabbed a can of water and poured it over the barrel of the .50 cal. It hissed with steam as the water streamed over it.

"Look!" I shouted.

Some of the men in our battalion's defensive emplacements had fixed bayonets to their rifles and were charging the Japanese on the beach. The two lines collided, and their screams were nearly louder than the gunfire. The fighting was hand to hand, fierce and ferocious.

Gunny looked down to see three boxes of ammo left for the .50 cal. If he shot the big gun now, he risked hitting our own troops. Instead, he picked up his rifle and snapped on the bayonet. "Let's go," he said. Jamison grabbed his rifle and did the same, firing on the run. I snapped the strap tight on my helmet, scrambled over the sandbags, and followed Gunny and Jamison, running in a zigzag pattern.

Planes were still strafing the beach, and bullets danced along the sand as I ran, some of them missing me by mere inches. As we reached the battle line, Gunny and Jamison disappeared in the crush of bodies.

But I couldn't follow them. A Japanese soldier crouched in front of me. I raised my rifle, pointed it at his chest, and pulled the trigger, but the gun did not fire. I had forgotten to rack a round into the chamber.

The man lurched forward and grabbed the rifle barrel as I tried desperately to work the bolt. We struggled and the gun slipped from my grasp, falling to the sand. The soldier grabbed my shirt and tried to throw me across his hip, but I was far too tall and he couldn't get the right leverage. We grappled and I tried to pull my knife, but it must have fallen out of the scabbard. He was shouting over and over, his mouth right next to my ear, but for some reason I could not hear him.

I felt something collide with my legs and landed hard on my back on the ground. I looked around for the rifle, but it was nowhere to be found. The soldier was suddenly on top of me, but I bucked and threw him off. We both scrambled to our feet and faced each other. I had no weapon, but the soldier wielded a small sword. With a scream he charged forward and I froze. But to my surprise the soldier spun away. A red flower of blood appeared in the middle of his chest as he tumbled to the ground.

I spun around to see Jamison holding his pistol, smoke coming from the barrel. He had no doubt just saved my life. "Look alive, Tree!" he shouted. "Gunny'll kill me if I let you die on my watch! Find a weapon! Stay right on my back."

I glanced about and spotted a rifle lying in the sand. I couldn't tell if it was mine or not, but right now it was finders, keepers. I picked it up and didn't even think to see if it was loaded or not. Just holding it made me feel better. Another Japanese soldier charged at me, and I pulled the trigger only to hear the rifle click. It was empty. *What was it with me and rifles?* I swung the rifle like a club, and the man went down. Then I pulled a clip from my ammo belt and snapped it home.

The noise of gunfire grew louder through the haze inside my brain and I gazed up to see Japanese fighter planes strafing the beach again. But this time two US warplanes—P-40 Warhawks—were engaging the enemy in the sky. I had no idea where they'd come from. The American pilots were outnumbered and outgunned, but they plunged into the fight. One of the Warhawks' machine guns ripped apart a Japanese Zero. The plane caught fire and plunged into the ocean. This brought a rousing cheer from our troops on the beach.

The fighting continued, hand to hand, and seemed to go on forever. Sometimes I felt like Jams was doing the fighting for both of us. I did what he said, sticking close to his side. He kept urging me on. “Heads up, Tree! Get in the fight! We’re gonna make it!” But even though he was standing right next to me most of the time, it felt like he was miles away.

Two more Warhawks arrived, and slowly the Japanese assault was beaten back. New explosions hit the beach as the tanks in the tree line fired. They had been held in reserve to save ammunition, but now they exacted a deadly toll on the Japanese forces.

“Fall back!” someone shouted. “Fall back!”

Fall back where? I wondered. Who was giving the order? There were still Japanese soldiers on the beach. As a bullet whizzed by my head, I stood frozen with indecision. Someone grabbed me by the neck, and I swung the rifle around only to find I’d just given Jamison a good thunk in the ribs.

“OW!” Jams yelled. “Move, Tree! Move! Move! You’re standin’ around like you wanna get shot. Follow me. Double-time it back to the ridge! Let’s go.”

I followed Jamison, who was running through and around the bodies and wreckage on the beach at full tilt.

We wove our way across the sand and somehow found the machine gun nest. Jamison grabbed a box of ammo and thrust it into my arms.

"You're gonna load," he said.

"Where's Gunny?" I asked.

"He'll get here when he gets here. Now let's go, Private!"

In a strange way, having a task to complete helped calm my nerves. I flipped open the lid on the metal box and pulled out the belt of machine gun bullets. Jamison was waiting. He slapped the belt across the magazine, snapped it shut, and swiveled the gun, firing in bursts whenever he found a target.

In the tree line the tanks were moving and firing, and it became clear we would repel this attack. Jamison swung the .50 cal back and forth, taking shot after shot. The belt ran out with a loud clang, signaling the gun was empty.

"Load!" Jamison shouted.

I grabbed the next belt and fed it into the gun, and Jamison resumed shooting. A few minutes later the gunfire died down. The Japanese planes had disappeared, and their landing barges had gone. Shouts of cease-fire came up and down the line. Jamison let go of the machine gun and turned, slumping against the sandbags. He ran his hands through his red hair. His face was covered in grime, and his white T-shirt was bloody where a cut on his chest was leaking.

"Jams, you're hurt," I said.

Jamison looked down at his chest and shrugged. "Just a scratch," he said.

"Where's Gunny?" I asked.

"I don't know, Tree. In case you didn't notice, it got a little bit nuts down there on the beach. Besides, it wasn't my turn to babysit him," Jamison said.

My face reddened. I lifted myself up to look over the emplacement, scanning the now darkened beach for any sign of Gunny. Jamison sighed.

"Look, kid. I'm sorry. I didn't mean to snap at you. It's just . . ."

"I know," I interrupted. "It's all right. I only—"

"You only what?" Gunny said as he flopped over the emplacement and slid in next to Jamison. In the pale moonlight, it looked like Gunny'd been wrestling a tornado and lost. His blouse was torn to shreds. There was a bloody cut above his right eye. Like Jamison, his face was nearly black with dirt and sweat.

"Gunny!" Jams and I shouted at the same time.

"What? Y'all think I was dead or somethin'? Uh-uh. Ain't no Imperial Japanese Army puke gonna kill Gunnery Sergeant Jack McAdams. I'm gonna live forever, boys, 'cause I'm just too dang handsome to get killed. Don't you worry, the good Lord ain't puttin' no early end to one of his finest creations. The worst thing happened out there was I lost my cigar. It was my last one, and no longer havin' it ain't improved my opinion of our Japanese friends any."

"What happened, Gunny?" Jamison said, offering him a cigarette.

The big man shrugged. "I don't reckon I know, Jamison. Not for sure. The enemy forces currently opposin' us did not invite me to their mornin' briefin'. I expect they'll try another attack some other place, seein' as how we're so well dug in here. But I do know we gotta hold this ground, because it's one of the best landing spots on this miserable hunk a rock." He took a puff on the cigarette and closed his eyes.

"You all right, Gunny?" I asked.

Gunny opened his eyes. "I'm fine. I dished out a lot more hurtin' than I took, I'll tell you that. But we got work to do. I got a feeling they's moving their battleships over yonder to the south. We know them planes is gonna be back. So the two of y'all dig in here. Make this hole deeper and see if you can scrounge up some more sandbags." He stood up, and I could see the exhaustion in his eyes.

"Shouldn't we keep moving?" I asked.

"Nah. This here spot has a natural depression and it's a fine defensive position. We'll keep it fer now. 'Sides they's gonna be more worried about our tanks and howitzers than a machine gun. If we have to we'll move it next time." He stood up.

"What are you gonna do?" Jamison asked.

"I'm gonna go see if I can find somebody in charge. Right now ain't nobody knows who's in command. Then I'm gonna try'n rustle us up some more ammo and rations. See if them tanks got any supplies they can spare. Get yer entrenchin' tools and make this emplacement at least three feet deeper. Once their ships start lobbin' shells on this beach, it'll make them bombers and fighter planes look like they was droppin' marshmallows."

He tossed the cigarette butt aside. "I'll be back soon as I can. When you finish, try'n get some shut-eye. I reckon y'all are gonna need it."

Gunny stood and removed a flashlight from his pack. He looked out over the beach and the ocean beyond. The hot breeze was back again, but the night was eerily quiet.

"It ain't over yet, boys. Not by a long shot."

He flipped on the flashlight and disappeared into the night. Jamison and I set to work.

"Well," Jamison said. "The next few days oughta be mighty interestin'."

CHAPTER FIVE

SURRENDER

The Japanese never came back to attack our beach. For months, their planes flew sorties over our positions and dropped bomb after bomb. They never seemed to run out. They never came at us on the beach, they never tried coming overland from Manila. It had now been almost four months since the Japanese first attacked the Philippines. After they took Manila, and the US forces retreated to Bataan and Corregidor, everyone figured we could hold out till help arrived. However, we soon realized Gunny'd been right. The Navy and General MacArthur—the commanding general of the Pacific forces who had hightailed it to Australia when the shooting started—weren't coming back anytime soon. They weren't even sending in planes or submarines to resupply the American positions.

We were on our own.

We stopped talking about reinforcements ever arriving. And we were almost out of food. Our remaining planes had been destroyed or were no longer flyable. Gunny stopped looking at the map every night. The Japanese were content to wait for the Allied forces on Bataan and Corregidor to starve.

We spent a lot of time making sure our weapons were clean and in working order and trying to scrounge up grub. At night, Jamison and I would sit with our backs against the sandbags, our rifles across our laps, and talk. Gunny would be off somewhere talking to other units, trying to find a working radio to get news, or trade for extra rations.

One night the stars were especially bright. And with the waves crashing in on the beach it was almost peaceful.

"You got a girlfriend back home, Tree?" he asked me.

"Huh . . . what . . . uh, no," I stammered.

Jamison chuckled. "Really? No special gal? Somebody at home pining for the day you come home?"

"No, Jams. I stopped going to school a few years ago, and girls just haven't been on my mind . . ."

"Oh, come on, Tree," he interrupted. "Not on your mind? I don't believe that."

"Well, I mean, yeah, I'd see girls in town . . . And there's a neighbor . . . Sandra . . . She's cute and all, but . . . I . . ."

"You're a smooth one, Tree," Jamison chuckled. "You ever kissed a girl?"

"Yeah. Of course."

"Liar."

"Well, what about you? If you're such a ladies' man. You have a girl back home?"

"In fact I do," he said, pulling a photograph from his blouse pocket. He handed it to me. I flipped on my flash-light and saw a pretty blond girl smiling out at me. She was dressed in a sweater and string of pearls.

"She's pretty," I said.

"Beautiful is what she is," he said. "When my hitch is up and I get back to Detroit, I'll get my job back at Dodge Main and we're gonna get married."

"Have you asked her yet?"

"Not yet." I handed him the photo, and he put it back in his pocket.

"How do you know she'll say yes?"

"Something wrong with your eyes, Tree? Haven't you seen the handsomeness and suavity that is me? No way she's gonna say no. I'm quite the catch."

I had to laugh. Jams was a cutup sometimes. He may have been a nervous and jerky kind of guy, which could be irritating, but you couldn't help but like him. When things got boring he'd always find a way to keep us laughing.

"Jams?"

"Yeah?"

"When the attack came and we were fighting on the beach . . . You saved my life. I never thanked you for it."

"Shoot, kid. That was nothin'. You'da done the same for me."

"I . . . I don't know about that, Jams. I was scared. Fired my gun probably two hundred times and I'm not sure I ever hit anything. It bothers me, being afraid all the time. How can I fight—be a Marine—if I'm always scared?"

"Everybody on this rock is afraid. Old Man Forsythe is probably so scared he can't remember none of his borin' stories. If he's still alive."

"You aren't, and neither is Gunny."

"Well, Gunny don't count, seein' as how he came down to earth from Olympus where they don't allow us mere mortals. But me? I'm scared. Anybody on this beach ain't scared, they're crazy."

"But you and Gunny just charged into the fight like you were going to the movies. I hesitated. I was . . . I was terrified."

"And what? You think that makes you a coward?"

"I don't know. Maybe."

"Tree, let me tell you somethin'. You ain't no coward. It was your first action. Think you're the only Marine ever froze up a little the first time bullets started flyin'? You got in there and fought, Tree. Like a man. You didn't cower in a foxhole. You followed me and Gunny right into the breach. Don't be so hard on yourself."

"I guess . . . It's just, I'm afraid of letting you both down."

"Well, I ain't worried about it. You answered the call. You'll do it again. It's time to give yourself a break. I don't know what makes you think you're some kind of coward or somethin', because you're the furthest thing from it." Jams stretched out and put his hands behind his head.

"I sure hope you're right."

"Tree, one thing you need to learn about me? I'm always right. We should try and get some shut-eye. Who knows when our friends are goin' to decide they wanna spend another day at the beach." Jams closed his eyes and was soon snoring softly. I was still too worried and nervous to sleep.

Jams and I spent a lot of nights like that. Talking about all sorts of things. It helped pass the time. But I soon found myself wishing the Japanese *would* attack. At least then something would happen. The boredom was unbearable.

Everyone's nerves were as frayed as an old piece of rope. Gunny did his best to keep our spirits up, but passing the hours in the machine gun nest was growing intolerable. Especially for Jamison, who started getting more and more jumpy as the days went by. One afternoon he finally cracked.

"I can't take this no more," he said. "I'm done." He stood and climbed out of the hole and up onto the ground.

"Where ya think yer goin,' Jams?" Gunny asked.

"I'm gettin' outta here. I'm gonna find me a boat and get off this rock," he said. He shrugged his pack onto his scrawny shoulders and grabbed his rifle.

"Good luck, then," Gunny said. "If you find one, come back and get me and Tree. We'll go with you."

Jamison muttered as he adjusted the straps on his pack. He cursed the Marines, the Army, the Navy, General MacArthur, President Roosevelt, Mrs. Roosevelt, the Japanese, and a bunch of other things I couldn't quite make out. Once he was ready, he set out toward the tree line.

"You think I should go get him, Gunny?" I asked.

"Nah," he answered. "He'll be back. Just goin' a little stir-crazy and burnin' off steam is all."

"What are we going to do, Gunny? I hate to keep asking, but isn't there somebody in charge with a plan?"

"There's only one man in charge when the shootin' starts. And his name is Jack Squat. Ain't nobody got a plan then, and if they do it's usually a poor excuse for one. We got caught with our pants down. Pearl. Guam. Wake. Here. The Japanese invaded China and Korea almost four years ago, and ain't nobody in the entire so-called US of A military intelligence stopped to think they might come here next? They been buildin' planes, tanks, subs, and ships for years, and it never occurred to one of yer so-called experts they might eventually take a poke at Uncle Sam? We wasn't ready. Not by a darn sight. No, Tree, there is no plan. Except survivin'."

"I heard a guy from the 104th Tank Battalion in the chow line this morning say we was getting evacuated to Corregidor."

"Evacuated in what?" Gunny said, pointing to the beachfront and the ocean beyond. "You see a fleet a troop transports out there ready to carry us away? We're sewed up tight. Boxed in. We ain't gettin' to Corregidor, and General Wainwright fer sure ain't comin' here."

Gunny leaned back against the sandbags and tipped his helmet over his eyes to block out the sun. General Wainwright had been left in charge of all Philippines defense forces when General MacArthur had left for

Australia. Wainwright was commanding from Corregidor. Working radios were in short supply, but from what we knew he and his forces were in no better shape than we were on Bataan.

"Sorry, Gunny. I didn't mean to get you riled up," I said.

"Ah, don't worry about it, kid. Yer a good Marine, Tree. And a good man. I just get the feelin' ya ain't figured that out yet, or more likely, as young as you are, ain't nobody ever told ya. But you've done good, kid. Course, you had the benefit of my trainin', which is a huge advantage fer even the below-average Marine."

I couldn't help but laugh.

"I almost wish they'd come back," I said.

Gunny raised his helmet and looked me straight in the eye.

"Believe me, boy, that is one thing ya don't want. Ever. Right now they's doing the smart thing. They know they got us. Why get a bunch of their men killed if they don't have to? They can drop bombs on us all day long. Make everybody as jumpy as a cat on roller skates. Old Yamamoto knows if reinforcements don't get here, all they gotta do is wait. They skirmish. Get us shootin' at their planes outta frustration, till we run out of ammo. Then they can walk right up the beach and all we'll be able to do is chuck coconuts at 'em. If we ain't ate all of 'em by then."

"Then what do we do?"

Gunny was quiet a minute. "We're makin' it out of here one of two ways. We're either goin' out feetfirst or wavin' the white flag. And to tell ya true, I ain't quite sure which way is best. The first way ain't nobody got no control over. But the other . . . Ya gotta find a place way down deep in yer soul. A place ain't nobody can go to but you. Not me, not Jamison, just you. And ya gotta make a promise when yer in that place to make it through whatever comes. No matter what happens to any other Devil Dogs stuck on this miserable patch of dirt. We're facin' an enemy that ain't just fightin' for land or rights or on account of we took somethin' belonged to 'em. We're fightin' 'em because they hate us. And if we surrender they's gonna hate us even more."

"What do you mean? Why would they hate us? If we surrender, don't they win?"

Gunny sat up and wiped his forehead with his arm. "With some other enemy maybe that'd be true. But the Japanese got a code. A buddy a mine worked maintenance with the Flyin' Tigers over in China before this shootin' match started. Says the Japanese don't believe in surrender.

Goes back to when they still had them samurai in the old days. It's called *Bushido*, and one of the rules of the code is 'no surrender.' They fight to the death. And when an enemy surrenders, it means they's less than human. Not worthy of honor or fair treatment or any of that other hooey. So if we surrender it's gonna get way worse than anything you seen on the beach. We've all gotta find a way to live through it, kid. Promise me. No matter what happens, ya gotta find a way."

I gulped, and as hot as it was, felt myself sweating even more. "I will, Gunny, I pro—"

I was interrupted by the abrupt return of Jamison. He came charging back into the foxhole, slid down the side of the sandbags, and landed in a heap.

"Tell me ya found a boat, Jams," Gunny said.

Jamison could hardly breathe. He'd obviously been running for a while.

"Word just came down, Gunny. Wainwright surrendered. We're to lay down arms."

PART TWO

THE DEATH MARCH

April 9, 1942

CHAPTER SIX

ARRIVAL

The order came down the line delivered in person by two ragged-looking officers, a colonel and a major, who moved from position to position, tank to tank, telling the soldiers we had officially surrendered.

Before our captors arrived, we set to work destroying all of the weapons and anything of strategic value we could. Gunny stripped down the .50 cal and threw the parts into the ocean. Tank crews set their machines on fire and broke the treads. The antiaircraft guns were scuttled. We may not have been fighting anymore, but we weren't going to allow the Japanese to use captured weapons.

The spot where we were dug in—on the southern end of the Bataan Peninsula—was called Mariveles. At the appointed time of the official surrender, the Japanese Army appeared unbelievably quickly. It was almost as if they'd been hiding in the trees. We were ordered to fall out and form into ranks. Japanese soldiers moved through our lines, taking weapons and searching us for valuables. That was when the first trouble started.

A Marine named Clarke, standing right in front of me, had a small Japanese flag in his pocket. The Japanese soldier searching him lost his mind when he found it. He drove the butt of his rifle hard into the Marine's stomach. The Marine grunted in pain and collapsed in a heap. He choked and gasped, scarcely able to breathe.

"NO!" I shouted, stepping forward to help him. As I did I found myself inches away from the Japanese soldier's bayonet. I stopped, my eyes locked on the man holding my fate in his hands. The soldier was shouting at me in Japanese, a look of pure hatred in his eyes.

"Tree," Gunny said quietly. "I ain't got the foggiest idea what he's sayin', but right now he's in a bad mood. Clarke will be okay. So stand back up in ranks, at attention. Remember what I said. Steady now."

Slowly, I stood up and returned to attention. Clarke groaned and tried rising to his feet. As he did, the soldier kicked him in the ribs, and Clarke went down again. Every muscle in my body tensed. I wanted to hurt that guard. I wanted to hurt him bad.

"Tree," Gunny whispered. "He's gonna be okay. I'm givin' you an order not to interfere."

Gunny's whispering drew the attention and ire of the Japanese soldier. He stepped over Clarke and got right up in Gunny's face. He spoke rapid-fire Japanese. It was impossible to understand what the man was demanding of us. But he clearly did not like us talking to each other. He finished his tirade and looked at Gunny as if waiting for an answer. When Gunny remained silent, he screamed the same words again. It must have been a question.

"Gunnery Sergeant Jack McAdams, serial number 040 187 0646," Gunny replied. Since basic training, we had been instructed to only give our name, rank, and serial number if we were ever captured. This was not what the Japanese soldier wanted to hear. His face turned red, and now his nose was inches away from Gunny's. Anger and rage filled his voice as he shouted at the sergeant again.

"I don't got the slightest idea what yer sayin', ya little pigheaded pile a dung," Gunny muttered. He kept his face impassive, not making eye contact with the man. The soldier thrust his hands into the pockets of Gunny's fatigues. He pulled out some cash and pocketed it. He tapped the other pocket with his bayonet and yelled something again.

Gunny understood then and emptied his pockets. He had a lighter, a letter from home, and a handkerchief.

I breathed a sigh of relief that there were no Japanese items in his pockets.

My relief was short-lived. The Japanese soldier turned his attention to me next. *I don't have anything in my pockets. I should—*

The blow came without warning. The rifle connected with the left side of my jaw. The pain felt like someone had taken a sledgehammer to my brain. I tasted blood in my mouth and sank to my knees. My eyes rolled up in my head, and I thought I might pass out. I heard Gunny cursing the Japanese soldier, who yelled and brandished his bayonet, preventing Gunny from coming to my aid.

"No . . . Gunny . . ." I mumbled. My mouth felt like it was full of marbles. My head sagged, and the world spun around me. I don't know how I managed to remain upright. Slowly I rose to one knee and then struggled back to a standing position. Woozy and dizzy, I wobbled until I could control myself enough to stand still.

"You okay, kid?" Gunny asked.

"Yeasth . . . I'm . . . all . . . fline," I said. My words were slurred, and my jaw was swelling. It took every bit of concentration and strength I had to keep standing. *Don't give in, Henry. Stand up. Push the pain down inside.* Gingerly I straightened further and returned to attention. Blood was filling my mouth, and some of it leaked out of the corner of my lips. Dizziness washed over me again and I was sure I was going to fall, but somehow I held on.

The Japanese soldier moved on to the man next to me. He was a member of the 173rd Fighter Squadron. I'd seen him around. He was a tall, blond, blue-eyed kid from Oklahoma. Baker or Baxter . . . or Banner. Banner was his name. A few years older than me, he was a quiet, keep-to-himself type.

Ever since we'd arrived in Bataan, all the battalions, regiments, and other units had been messed up. There were so many men killed and wounded, command tried mixing everybody together to make up some semblance of a fighting force. We were all on the same side, but unless you were able to stay with members of your original unit, like I'd gotten to with Gunny and Jams, it was hard to get to know each other well with everyone being moved around and reassigned all the time. In a lot of cases, you ended up fighting alongside guys you didn't know.

The Japanese soldier was searching Banner. He took money, a small Bible, and a St. Christopher's medal from the pocket of Banner's fatigues. The Japanese soldier dropped the Bible and medal on the ground and stomped on them, grinding them into the dirt.

The Japanese guard was about to move on when he spied something sticking out of the pilot's blouse pocket. He roughly removed it and found another small Japanese flag. It was torn and covered in bloodstains. At the sight of it, he lost all control. He shouted at Banner, waving the flag in front of his face. Banner remained silent, but he was trembling. The soldier thrust the butt of his rifle straight into Banner's chin, and he fell to the ground. Then the rifle swung again, connecting with the back of Banner's head with a sickening thud.

I tensed, my muscles coiled. I would rather go down fighting than watch the Japanese beat my fellow soldiers senseless. Just as I was about to spring, Gunny took hold of my arm. It felt like a bear trap had closed over it. I couldn't move if I wanted to.

"Tree!" he whispered. "*At ease, Marine.* Don't move a muscle. That's an order, ya understand me?"

Hearing us, our tormentor spun, holding the rifle at his waist, the metal bayonet gleaming in the sun. He shouted at us, waving it back and forth.

"I'm gonna turn you loose. But don't move. I mean it, Tree," Gunny said.

I relaxed, and Gunny released his grip. I tried not looking at the Japanese soldier holding the rifle. I couldn't fathom how someone could be so full of hate. This guy seemed worse than my father. At least my dad didn't get this mean until he got all liquored up. I tried not looking at this hate-filled man, but I couldn't stop staring.

Though Gunny was standing right next to me, his voice sounded far away. "Tree! Quit starin' at the little weasel."

The Japanese soldier smiled at me. It was an angry, vicious smile. His teeth were crooked, and he had a long scar along his right cheek. *All right, Scarface,* I thought. *You win this round.* I turned and tried focusing on something in the distance.

It was almost like the soldier could read my mind. He spat at me and pivoted back to Banner, who still lay on the ground. He raised his rifle, then drove the bayonet through Banner's back.

This time not even Gunny could stop me. "Noooo!" I screamed.

I flew through the air, colliding with the soldier, and we both tumbled to the ground. The guard couldn't free the bayonet from the body, but he was a slippery snake. One minute I was on top of him, raising my fist to punch him in the head. The next, he flipped me over him with his legs, quick as a cobra. He was stronger than he looked.

I landed hard on my head and chest, rolled over, and jumped to my feet.

Now the soldier had the rifle back. He charged at me, and I sidestepped him. I could hear Gunny yelling at me to stand down, but the soldier had a mind to kill me. I grabbed the barrel of his gun and we struggled, until he was able to jerk away from me. Then he reared back and cracked me hard on the side of the head with his rifle.

That was the last clear memory I had for quite a while.

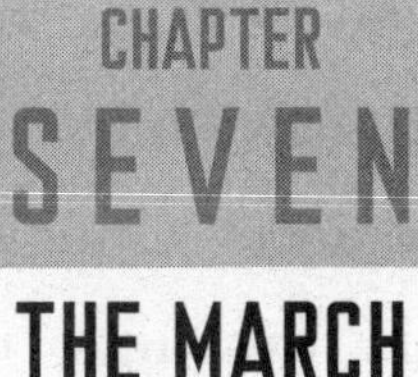

CHAPTER SEVEN

THE MARCH

My eyes fluttered as I came to. Gunny was leaning over me. "Tree . . . Tree . . . Can you hear me, boy?" he said. He gently slapped my cheek. "Come on now. I need ya to wake up, son. Let's go."

My eyes finally opened, but I shut them immediately. I couldn't focus, and they rolled up in my head. I almost vomited. My jaw and the entire side of my head throbbed with each heartbeat. It was impossible to tell if I was lying on the ground or sitting up. The world seemed upside down.

"Tree, c'mon now, boy. Ya in there?" I felt water on my lips. As if it had a mind of its own, my tongue darted out of my swollen lips and slurped at the water. It felt like heaven in my mouth, and I gulped it down.

"Attaboy. C'mon, wake up now." I heard a clicking sound. Opening my eyes let in too much sunlight, making me squint. But Gunny was snapping his fingers in my face.

"Wha . . . happen . . . ?" I muttered. My tongue felt thick and awkward, and speaking was difficult. My head throbbed, and blood thundered in my ears.

"What do ya remember?" Gunny asked.

"Whew . . ." I said, exhaling. "I don't remember . . . any . . . Where's Jamison?"

"I don't know," Gunny said. He was holding my eyelids open and checking my pupils. "I hope ya ain't got a concussion. That was one stupid move, going all ninja on that duly authorized representative of the Imperial Japanese Army the way ya did."

One sliver of memory came flooding back. The Japanese soldier stabbed Banner in the back, and I jumped him. Everything after that was gone.

"What happened?"

"What happened? What happened, *Private*, is first ya disobeyed my direct order to stand down. Second, as a result of that insubordination, ya got the livin' tar beat outta ya," Gunny said. "I ain't never seen a body do somethin' so stupid. Yer lucky to be alive. It took every ounce of convincin' I had in me to keep 'em from killin' ya. The next time I give an order, ya better follow it."

I opened my eyes a little further. I was leaning against a palm tree. Gunny held out the canteen, and I drank deeply.

"Hold up there," Gunny said, pulling the water away. "I know yer thirsty, but our new friends here don't seem all that hospitable. So we better save as much water as we can."

"Where's Jamison?" I asked again.

"I don't know, Tree. They separated us into a bunch a different groups. Everybody got moved around. Wherever he is, he's probably fine. Jams knows what's what. He'll be okay. Turns out it's you we gotta watch out for."

"I'm fine, Gunny. Really. We need to go find Ja—" I tried standing up and would have keeled over if Gunny hadn't caught me. My vision spun again, and Gunny gently lowered me to the ground.

"We ain't goin' nowhere till ya come back to yer senses," Gunny said. I glanced around. Everywhere I looked, American and Filipino prisoners sat on the ground. Around us, Japanese soldiers stood every few yards with their weapons at the ready.

"What do you think is gonna happen?" I asked.

"Don't know. Right now I'm just hopin' they don't shoot us," Gunny answered.

"They wouldn't do that, would they?"

"Ya see what they done to that pilot next to ya? Why wouldn't they do the same to us? Be a whole lot less trouble for 'em."

I had never considered that. The image of Banner being stabbed in the back was slowly returning to me. Maybe Gunny was right. Maybe our enemies didn't follow the rules. I scanned the faces of the Japanese guards. All of them looked tense and angry.

"But you must have some idea, Gunny?"

"Well, it's clear to me yer feeling better on account of how ya won't quit with the questions. I ain't got a clue what they got planned for us. Maybe when they find out I'm an actual gunnery sergeant, they'll take me into their confidence and I'll be able to fill ya in."

For hours we sat in the hot sun. Whenever the men grouped together, the Japanese soldiers would separate them, prodding them with their rifles and bayonets, keeping the prisoners spread out. Some of the guards were rougher than the others. Men sitting quietly were unexpectedly and without warning beaten with rifles or wooden rods for no reason that I could see. Luckily me and Gunny were in the middle of the group, next to a palm tree. None of the guards paid us any attention. I wondered what happened to the one who had killed Banner. I tried, but I could barely remember his face. *A scar. He had a scar. And crooked teeth. Scarface.* That was all I could recall through the haze. I didn't see him anywhere nearby. *Hope he didn't hurt anybody else*, I thought.

As my senses slowly returned, I scanned the crowd hoping to see Jamison, but could not locate him in the teeming mass of men. With nothing else to do but think, I was reminded again of all the reasons why I wished I'd never come to the Philippines. The air was thick with humidity, like a wet blanket constantly covering us. The breeze was miserably hot, and were it not for the pitiful shade of the palm tree, the sun would set our skin to sizzling like bacon on a grill.

But I'd made my choice when I lied and joined up. The Marine Corps was not a democracy. You got sent where you got sent. Right now, despite the unrelenting brightness of the sun, it felt as if I were in the darkest corner of the world.

I dozed with my back to the tree and had no idea how much time had passed. It must've been a few hours later when a Japanese staff car arrived, followed by a small convoy of trucks filled with more Japanese soldiers. An officer emerged from the back of the car. He was dressed in an immaculate uniform, carrying a riding crop in his hand and wearing knee-high leather boots.

The guards herded us prisoners toward the car. The officer was there to speak to us and wanted to be sure he was heard. Me and Gunny rose to our feet. I was still wobbly and unsteady. Gunny took me by the arm to keep me from pitching over.

When the officer was satisfied everyone was within hearing distance, he smacked the riding crop into his open hand. He stared at the assembly of prisoners, his gaze traveling slowly over us, his face a mask of contempt. He looked arrogant and mean. The man unnerved me a little bit.

It shocked all of us when he spoke in perfect English.

"My name is Major Sato of the Imperial Japanese Army. You are our prisoners. It is only through the generosity of His Holiness the Emperor that you are not lying dead on the field of battle. Through his graciousness, you will be treated fairly and humanely as long as you follow the commands that we, his servants, make on his behalf. Disobeying us is disobeying the emperor, and is punishable by death. You are captives. You do not have rights. Some of your officers have complained to me that your treatment is a violation of the Geneva Convention on the rules of war. I am here to tell you that the Empire of Japan is greater than all other nations. We do not recognize the Geneva Convention, nor are we bound by it. The only rules to be followed are the ones we decide. If you comply, you have nothing to fear. If you do not . . ." He let his words trail off.

I wondered how he spoke such excellent English and got my answer quickly.

"I am a graduate of Harvard University. I returned to my homeland to serve the Emperor. In America, I learned that your society is lazy, corrupt, and slovenly. Our defeat of your military will be complete. For now, you will do nothing else but follow orders. You will complete whatever task you are instructed to do without hesitation or complaint. If you do not, your punishment will be swift and severe. Prisoner quarters are now being prepared at Camp O'Donnell on the northern end of Bataan. You will march there. You will not delay. If you try to escape, you will be shot. If you attempt to delay or disrupt the march in any manner, you will be shot. That is all."

Major Sato returned to the car, and it pulled away. The troops that had arrived in trucks moved into position. They started yelling and giving orders that no one could understand. Finally, someone figured out we were to form a column and prepare to march.

"Ya gonna be able to march, Tree?" Gunny asked.

"I think so. I got a headache won't quit and I wish someone would turn off the sun. But I'll make it."

They formed us in a long column, four abreast. Gunny stood to my left on the outside of the rank. I stood next to two men I didn't know. I heard them whispering something about Camp O'Donnell. But before I could ask them what they knew, the order came down the line, "Column! March!"

Slowly, rank by rank, the entire group of American prisoners shuffled forward on the dusty road. I thought about what I'd just overheard. All I knew about Camp O'Donnell was that it was more than sixty miles away. I couldn't believe the Japanese would have us march the entire distance. Many of the men were wounded. They would never make it that far.

After a few hours of marching in the hot sun, I grew dizzy and faint. Gunny carefully parceled out the water from his canteen, but it didn't help. Now that I was upright and moving, I realized more than just my head and jaw were hurting. My ribs ached, and my right knee was beginning to swell. I must have taken a horrible beating after jumping the guard that killed Banner.

I glanced at Gunny. He'd removed his blouse and tied it over his head to shield him from the sun. I noticed for the first time that he looked a little roughed up, too. His right arm was hanging stiff at his side. He was also walking with a slight limp. I wondered if he'd been injured protecting me in the fight. *If he got those injuries saving me, I'll never forgive myself,* I thought.

On we marched. Hours passed. The sun and the heat were cruel masters, driving men to their knees in exhaustion. The column in front of us kicked up clouds of dust, and we in the rear coughed and choked on it. The wounded lagged behind. Whenever they did, one of the Japanese guards would punish them with a rifle butt to the small of the back or a kick to the midsection. Every time it happened, I heard Gunny quietly curse them as cowards.

Soon the long column splintered and broke apart. Some of the men were too badly injured to keep up. Any sign of weakness was an invitation for the Japanese to abuse the sick and suffering even more. Sometimes I could scarcely believe what I witnessed. Men so badly hurt they tumbled to the ground. When they did the Japanese fell on them, kicking and screaming at them to keep moving. Some of them were able to summon the strength to climb to their feet again. But others could not. I tried to forget what happened to them. I felt like it would haunt me forever.

A few hours later, a young Marine two rows in front of us collapsed in the dusty road. He had a serious head wound. An older Marine walking next to him stooped to lift him to his feet. The row in front of us simply moved around them, but I took the fallen man's other arm, and between me and the older guy, we got the sick man up and walking.

"What's your name, Marine?" my partner asked.

"Private Henry Forrest. But everybody calls me Tree," I said.

"I appreciate the help. I'm First Lieutenant Newbery. This here is Martinez. We're from the 8th Marine Division."

"Pleasure to meet you, sir," I said.

"Where you from, Forrest?" Newbery asked.

"Minnesota."

"Minnesota, ay? I'm from Cody, Wyoming. What about you, Gunny?" the lieutenant asked, glancing at the stripes on Gunny's blouse hanging from his head.

Gunny looked straight ahead and didn't reply at first. "Denton, Texas," he finally answered. He had an uneasy look on his face. More and more men fell out of the column. Their comrades tried to help, but many could barely march themselves. One after another we watched as men collapsed to the ground in exhaustion. We could do nothing to help them.

"Tree," Gunny whispered. "I don't got a good feelin' about this. Heads up. Keep yer eyes forward and don't start no trouble."

"What is it, Gunny?" Lieutenant Newbery asked.

"I ain't sure. Them Japanese keep clusterin' up and talkin' to each other like they got somethin' on their mind. I don't care for the look of it," Gunny said.

"Surely they're only—"

Before I could finish, a group of Japanese soldiers approached the wounded Americans who lay wearily on the ground. I watched, horrified, as one of the guards raised his rifle and pulled the trigger, shooting one of the injured men. Another calmly stabbed a downed man in the chest with his bayonet. The other prisoners raised their hands and pleaded for their lives, but the guards moved from man to man shooting or stabbing each one.

"My God!" the lieutenant muttered.

"Sir," Gunny said, "I don't reckon God's around right now."

CHAPTER EIGHT

DESCENT

Onward we marched. After a time, I was convinced the brutality I'd witnessed was all a dream. Instinct had taken over, and my body simply put one foot in front of the other. Two other Marines took turns helping Martinez along. Sullivan was a tall, big guy with blond hair and ruddy cheeks. "Everybody calls me Sully. How original," he laughed. He was from Los Angeles. Worthy was a smaller guy, black hair and dark eyes that never stopped moving. He said he was from Kentucky, and he spoke with a thick southern drawl. But actually, he didn't say much else. His eyes darted everywhere. It was hard to blame him, given the situation we were in. All of us, including the lieutenant, took turns carrying Martinez along.

We had finished the last of Gunny's water miles back. The sun was sinking low in the sky, but the heat and humidity remained. Thirst became the enemy, and it overwhelmed all of us quickly. I lost track of how many men dropped out of the column. Of the number slain by the

Japanese when they collapsed in the dirt or were unable to keep marching. Some made the mistake of begging for water and received horrible beatings for their trouble.

As darkness descended, the column arrived at a deserted fuel dump along the road. A chain-link fence enclosed it, but it was too small to hold all of the remaining prisoners. That made no difference to the Japanese, who pushed and shoved us into the enclosure. Some of the prisoners pushed back, which only made the Japanese beat them with their rifles and clubs. Finally our captors jammed everyone inside. There was no room to lie down or sit. Dirty, thirsty, dying men leaned against each other whether they wanted to or not.

Gunny stuck next to me. "How ya hangin', kid?" he asked.

"I'm okay, Gunny."

"Liar."

My left eye had swollen shut, and my teeth were loosened where the rifle had connected with my jaw. I still felt woozy, with no idea how I managed to make it this far. All I wanted was a place to lie down.

Finally, some of the officers got organized and rearranged the prisoners until there was enough room for some of the most seriously wounded to rest on the ground.

There were no doctors in our group, but there were a few medical corpsmen. They didn't have any supplies, but they treated the injured the best they could. Sweat-soaked shirts were torn into bandages. Any water that was left among us cleaned wounds and was given to the weakest and most injured to drink.

All during the night, the Japanese patrolled the fence. When the morning sun rose, fourteen more men had died in the night. It made no difference to the Japanese. They opened up our cage and ordered us to march. The dead were left behind.

After hours of walking, we arrived at the San Fernando rail station. A train waited with perhaps a dozen boxcars. Prisoners were loaded on and jammed inside. Just when I thought there was no room on a car, the Japanese would force another ten or twelve men inside. I counted more than a hundred crammed into a single boxcar, packed so tight the doors would barely shut. Finally it was me and Gunny's turn. A couple of surly guards with bayonets on their rifles stood by the door, yelling at us to climb aboard.

"Gunny," I said, my voice all nervous and crackly. "I can't do this. I can't take it."

"Stow that talk, Private," Gunny said, his voice hoarse and gravelly.

"No, Gunny . . . I mean it—"

"Private Forrest, I just ordered ya to shut yer trap. I don't care if they put two hundred of us in that boxcar, yer gonna take it. Dig down deep, Private. Down inside to the absolute bottom of yer soul. I don't want to hear nothin' 'bout can't. Am I clear?"

"Yeah, Gunny . . . I . . . guess . . ."

"I don't deal in guesses, Tree. Do whatever it is ya need to get through this. Count to two thousand. Then count to three thousand. Go minute by minute until it adds up to an hour. Find something to take yer mind off of where ya are. Clear?"

"Yeah, Gunny, loud and clear." My mouth was so dry I could barely get the words out. The sun had risen over the horizon and beat down on us. But it was going to be a lot hotter inside. Finally the Japanese soldiers herded us into the boxcar. I thought the fenced-in fuel depot from the previous night was crowded, but it was nothing compared to the boxcar.

Men jostled and yelled at each other, driven mad by thirst and exhaustion. After the cars were loaded the train rolled down the track. As it picked up speed the jerking motion caused more and more men to bump into each other. The ride was anything but smooth, but it was better than marching. I hoped when the ride ended we'd be taken to a barracks or someplace where we could rest and get food and water.

But that was not to be.

The railway ended at Capas in the province of Tarlac. We were herded off the train, and it departed the way we had come. There was still no food or water provided. Then came the order to march again. After a short time we arrived at the gates of Camp O'Donnell. The former military base had been turned into a prisoner of war camp. Outside the gate a ditch was filled with brackish, muddy water. The sight of the water drove many of the men wild. They couldn't resist and stampeded forward, sliding down the embankment, where they gulped down mouthfuls of the dirty liquid. I moved to follow them, but Gunny clamped a hand over my arm.

"No, Tree," he said.

"Let me go, Gunny. Please. I'm dying of thirst."

"Drink that water and ya *will* die. It ain't safe. Besides . . ."

His words trailed off as we watched the guards pulling the men out of the ditch and back into the column. Some of them were so mad with thirst they fought the Japanese and were either beaten or bayoneted for their troubles.

Soon the ditch filled with dead bodies. The prisoners who were still breathing were forced back into the column.

The guards marched hundreds upon hundreds of captives inside the gates. The Japanese had enclosed the camp with fences topped with coils of barbed wire. Other prisoners were already there, including hundreds of Filipino civilians and Philippine scouts. In no short time, the camp grew impossibly crowded. The Japanese had vastly underestimated the number of survivors.

But at long last, there was drinkable water. Or rather, a chance at water. In the center of the camp was a well. Several hoses with water trickling out of them drew the prisoners like a wolf to a pork chop. The hoses became another battleground, as men shoved and pushed and fought each other. Finally exhaustion seemed to grasp hold of the entire group, and a ragged set of lines formed at each hose.

Gunny stood in front of me, and when he reached the front of the line, he filled his canteen and handed it back to me. Gunny drank directly from the hose while I guzzled the water from the canteen. It was warm and dirty, but I never tasted something so good in my life. I was still focused on the water rushing into my mouth when Gunny crashed into me. Another soldier had shoved him out of the way, yanking the hose out of his hand.

"Gimme that! No hoggin' the water!" the man yelled at him.

Gunny straightened and sized up the man, who was filthy, dressed in a tattered army blouse, with corporal's stripes on his sleeve. His lips were cracked and bleeding. With dark eyes he glared at Gunny while he drank deeply from the trickling water.

Gunny's hand shot out and grabbed the man around the neck. With one hand he lifted him off the ground. The man yelped and dropped the hose. His eyes bugged out of his head. His dirty fingers clawed at Gunny's iron grip, but it was useless. Gunny was not letting go.

"What's yer name, Corporal?" Gunny demanded.

"Grimes. Corporal Grimes. 7th Artillery Battalion. Lemme go," the man gasped, his face turning blue.

Gunny released his grip, and Grimes inhaled, sucking in a great, ragged breath. Gunny stepped up to the man, his face inches away from Corporal Grimes's nose.

"I'm *Gunnery* Sergeant Jack McAdams, 15th Infantry, United States Marine Corps. Don't ever lay a hand on me again. Ya understand me? Not a finger. Or I'll bite it off. We clear?"

Corporal Grimes was coughing and gagging, but he nodded.

"C'mon, Tree," Gunny said after he refilled the canteen. I followed him, but not before noticing the hard, evil look Grimes was giving him.

"You might have just made an enemy, Gunny," I said.

"Well, he'll need to get himself in line behind the Japanese. I suspect we're gonna have a lotta enemies before this is over, Tree."

We found a spot outside of a barracks wall that was now in the shade and sat down in the dirt leaning against it. Both of us groaned as we sat. Gunny took another sip from the canteen.

"Ya see them Japanese out there with the guns, Tree," he said, pointing to the guards patrolling the fence.

"Yeah, I see 'em."

Gunny leaned back against the barracks wall and closed his eyes. "Them's our enemy. We gonna have a lot more to worry about'n some thirsty artillery corporal," he said. "Trust me on that."

PART THREE

CAPTIVITY

1942

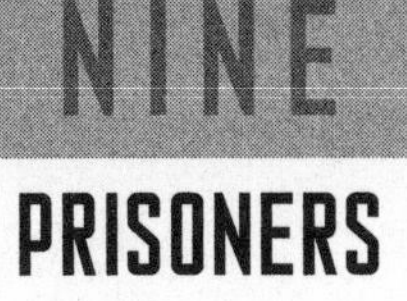

CHAPTER NINE

PRISONERS

The camp was a chaotic mess. After a time, prisoners were roughly assigned to barracks by unit and nationality. But there were too many of us and not enough English-speaking guards to organize everything efficiently. We ended up in a three-sided open barracks with Sully, Worthy, Martinez, and a few other men. We all shuffled into the building, picked a spot by the wall, and slid down to the floor, too exhausted to talk.

I could tell Gunny was sticking close, watching out for me. But the fact we had yet to find Jamison worried me. I had a feeling something bad had happened to him. Jamison had a temper. Usually Gunny was good at keeping him under control. But there were times, before the invasion, when Jams and I would be out on our own, that he would get into fights and end up in the brig. Gunny could usually do a favor for one of the MPs or smooth things over so Jamison didn't get in too much trouble. But those days were long gone now. Jams had saved my life on the beach. He watched out for me, just like Gunny did. I needed to know what had happened to him. But right now, I was too tired, hungry, and weak to search the compound. I huddled next to Gunny, my back against the barracks and every part of me aching. For the next few hours, I scanned the face of every man that passed by, but I did not see Jamison.

An area just inside the gate had been taken over by those too injured or sick to assign to a barracks. Dozens of bodies littered the ground. There were too many for me to count. I wondered if Jamison might be among them. I nudged Gunny with my elbow. He came awake with a start.

"What's wrong?" he said.

"Nothing. I'm going to take a walk over by the wounded and see if I can find Jamison. I'm worried about him. You stay here and rest until I get back," I said.

"Kid, I told ya. No need to worry about Jamison . . ."

"I know, Gunny. I can't help it. I'll be careful."

I was so weak I needed to use the wall to raise myself up to a standing position. My head ached, and I groaned as I shuffled toward the large group of injured men. I counted at least two hundred men lying in the dirt. Some of them might already be dead. Their bodies were still and lifeless. At least this time there were a couple of doctors around, along with medical corpsmen. They were doing the best they could with what they had. But the Japanese had given them no medicine, no supplies. Major Sato hadn't been kidding. Japan definitely didn't follow the Geneva Convention. It appeared they didn't care if their prisoners died or not.

I walked slowly among the rows of dead and wounded, studying the face of each man.

"Jamison? Jams? You here?" I called out.

No one paid attention to me. After a while I stopped. Some of the men had been beaten so severely I thought I wouldn't have recognized Jamison even if I'd found him. The variety of wounds was sickening. Men had been stabbed, shot, and clubbed, and in some cases it looked as if a few of them had been burned. Some had no visible wounds, but merely looked broken from exhaustion.

I still hadn't found Jamison, and dark thoughts crept into my mind. I pictured him on the dusty road, standing up to some Japanese soldier and being shot or stabbed. My mind wouldn't let go of the awful images.

Lost in thought, I wasn't paying attention when I bumped into a medical corpsman.

"Can I help you?" the man said, his voice irritable.

"Sorry. I'm looking for my friend. His name is Billy Jamison. He's a corporal in the 15th Marine Infantry. We got separated on the march. You haven't seen anybody by that name, have you?" I asked.

"Yeah. Six Jamisons. Fourteen Tuckers and seven Smiths," the man said sarcastically. "How in heck would I know? Most of these men ain't even wearin' dog tags, and about one hundred percent of 'em ain't in any shape to talk. If your friend is here, all you're doing is getting in our way. Let us do our jobs, and you can look for your friend later."

"Sorry," I said. I started to return to the barracks, and was just about to the end of the row when a hand shot out and grabbed my ankle.

"Tree?" the man croaked.

I stopped and glanced down at a face that hardly looked human. The nose was bent to the side, broken and twisted. One eye was completely swollen shut. His lips were split and bleeding.

"Jamison?" I said. "Is that you?"

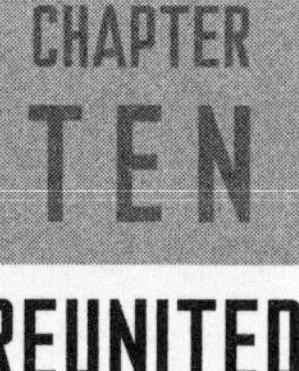

CHAPTER TEN

REUNITED

I dropped to my knees next to Jams—kicking up a cloud of dust—and closely examined his injuries. The poor guy had been beaten until he was practically unrecognizable. For a moment, I was overcome with rage, wanting nothing more than to find whoever had done this to him and make them pay for it.

I gently touched his face, and Jamison winced. "Sorry, Jams," I said, quickly pulling my hand away. "What happened? Are you all right?"

"I'm right as rain," Jamison croaked. "I don't s'pose you got a fresh cig, do ya? Be nice to have a smoke while I'm enjoyin' this lovely tropical climate."

"Dang it, Jamison, quit joking around and tell me what happened!"

"I got into a minor disagreement with three, maybe four members of the Imperial Japanese Army. They took a decidedly negative view of my complainin' over their ungentlemanly treatment of some of my fellow servicemen.

And the lot of 'em, well, they decided to kick me in the head, face, and other assorted intensely sensitive areas on my person."

"You look awful."

"Awful—" Jamison was interrupted by a phlegmy, racking cough that sounded horrible. I wondered if he had broken ribs. But when he caught his breath he was chuckling. "Believe me. That don't come nowhere near close to describin' how I feel."

Jamison closed his one good eye and groaned in pain.

I took hold of his shoulders. "Jams! What's wrong?" I looked around. "Corpsman! I need help here!" I shouted.

A medic tending to a soldier in the next row looked at me and shrugged. "You're going to have to wait your turn, pal. As you can see, the waitin' room is kind of full."

I took hold of Jamison and cradled him in my arms. He shuddered and groaned in the throes of some kind of seizure. I tried grasping him tight against my chest to keep him from shaking. But then I grew afraid I'd squeeze too hard and hurt him worse. I gently laid Jamison back on the ground.

"Jams! I'll be right back. I'm going to get Gunny. He's got a canteen of water, and he'll know what to do. I'll be right back, I promise."

Jamison said nothing. He was in the midst of whatever had overtaken him, twisting, writhing, and moaning on the ground. I was still banged up, and I moaned as I climbed to my feet. As fast as I was able, I scrambled back toward the barracks, where Gunny was waiting. I desperately wanted to run, but I was in far too much pain and my legs weren't working right. I was still exhausted from the march. But I shuffled as fast as I could.

I spied Gunny right where I'd left him, eyes closed dozing against the wall. Just as I was about to call out, I tumbled to the ground. It took a brief moment to sink in, but then an excruciating pain in my shins traveled up my legs, and I writhed on the ground, screaming in agony. When the pain subsided and I could focus again, I glanced up to find a shadowy figure blocking out the sun. It was so bright I was unable to see the man's face. Then I was roughly jerked to my feet.

A Japanese soldier stood facing me holding a wooden club. A scar traveled down his face from his forehead, across his eye, ending at his lip. When the man smiled at me, his teeth were chipped and crooked.

It was the same guard. Scarface. The one who had beaten me the day we surrendered. I could do nothing but watch as the man strengthened his grip on the club and raised it over his head. The blow connected, rocking me to my core and further injuring my already beat-up ribs.

I was about to cry out when the words Gunny said to me before the surrender flashed into my mind. About how things were going to get worse before all of this was over. How I would need to dig down deep to survive. It would be the hardest thing I'd ever done. But Gunny believed in me. He told me I was strong enough to endure what was coming.

And in that briefest of moments, I swallowed the cry in my throat. All that escaped was a small grunt. The Japanese guard looked down at me and sneered. He clearly remembered who I was. With another vicious smile he raised his club and reared back again. It whistled through the air, connecting with the back of my shoulders like a baseball bat hitting a side of beef.

The blow drove me to my hands and knees. The pain was excruciating, but though I desperately wanted to cry out in pain, I refused to let any noise escape. The guard watched, waiting to see what I would do next. I gathered myself and slowly, with great effort, climbed to my feet. I kept my face calm and expressionless.

"Is that all you got?" I asked. Taunting him helped give me something to focus on. It stopped me from giving in to the agony.

The guard stared at me, his eyes narrowed.

"Is that all you got?" I repeated, louder this time.

The guard drove the butt of his stick into my stomach. The force of the blow doubled me over, and I felt the vomit rising in my throat. But I choked it back down. *Survive it, Tree.*

Slowly, I stood up straight. Forced myself to stay calm. I glared back at the guard, and then I smiled. My lips were swollen and bloody, and I imagined I looked like an evil clown.

"I'm going to get help for my friend," I said. "You can beat me all you want. It won't stop me." I took a step around the guard and collapsed in the dust again when the club connected with the back of my knees. I fell face forward into the dirt. *Don't cry out. Don't make a sound.* I demanded it of myself. I kept the thoughts running through my mind, refusing to think of anything else.

Slowly, purposefully, I placed my hands on the ground. One knee at a time, I rose up. With all of my strength I stood. The guard's expression had changed. He stared at me with a face cloaked in curiosity. As if he couldn't figure me out. Why was this Yank not succumbing to his punishment? Why was he not cowering in fear?

"All right, *Scarface*," I said. "You want to belt me again, go ahead. You hit like a girl anyway."

Though he didn't speak English, the guard understood that he was being challenged or insulted. The idea that I would attempt to take the power away from him was more than he could tolerate.

With both hands on the club, he wound up to deliver a crushing blow. I braced for the collision. *No matter how bad it hurts, don't show anything. Don't. Show. Anything,* I told myself.

A loud shout in Japanese brought the guard to an immediate halt. I turned to see a Japanese officer issuing some kind of order. Apparently the guard was needed somewhere else, and they both ran off together.

I let out a sigh of relief. *I'll see you later, Scarface. I'll definitely see you later.*

Slower and bent slightly with fresh pain, I shuffled off to get Gunny.

CHAPTER ELEVEN

LIVING

It took every bit of strength we had, but Gunny and I finally managed to carry Jamison to our spot in the barracks. The seizure or whatever it was had passed, but Jams was still in bad shape. Gunny got him to drink a few sips of water from the canteen. He ripped a piece off his blouse, soaked it in water, and dabbed at the cuts on Jamison's face.

"Ow," Jamison yelled, the pain bringing him back to a level of semiconsciousness. "Why sure, Gunny, that don't hurt at all. Not even a tiny little bit. Where'd you learn your first aid? Did you even read the field manual?"

"Shut yer trap, Corporal Jamison. Yer lucky *I* don't give you a worse beatin'. What were you thinkin'? Takin' on three Japanese soldiers . . ."

"I guess you could say I wasn't thinkin'. Not with a clear head anyhow. Last thing I remember is three of 'em using their bayonets, makin' a pincushion out of this infantryman in the rank ahead of me as we were marchin'. It was *sick* is what it was. They kept stabbin' him and he kept bleedin', but they weren't stickin' him anywhere that'd kill him. It was like they wanted to see how long they could make him bleed and how much pain they could cause. He kept beggin' 'em to stop, but they wouldn't. They were laughin'. I think it was the most gruesome thing I ever seen. He was screamin', and it finally got to the point where he couldn't walk. He fell down in the dirt, and I knew they were going to kill him. That's when I politely asked them to refrain from murdering my brother-in-arms. One of them rushed me. I think I got in a couple of pretty good licks at first. But the next thing I know, they'd pushed me down, and all three of 'em were practicin' their karate or judo or whatever you call it, in the general vicinity of my head. Next thing I remember, old Tree here was walkin' by."

"Jamison, yer lucky to be alive," Gunny muttered. "I give ya marks, Corporal. Yer one tough hombre and stubborn as a mule. But just as stupid. We ain't gonna live through this if we keep provokin' them guards."

"I don't know, Gunny," Jamison said. "Provokin' people is about the only talent I got." He coughed again and winced, holding his ribs.

Gunny probed Jamison's ribs with his fingers.

"Ow," Jamison winced. "Gunny, I know you mean well, an' please don't take this the wrong way, but you really need to brush up on your doctorin' skills."

"Probably got yer ribs busted," Gunny said, ignoring Jamison's jibe. "Tree, give me yer T-shirt."

I pulled my sweaty blouse over my head. Gunny ripped it into a long strip.

"I'm gonna have to wrap yer ribs, and it's gonna hurt like you just stuck yer head in a hornet's nest. Tree'll hold up yer arms."

As gently as I could, I lifted Jamison's arms over his shoulders. Jamison tried not to groan and failed. Gunny wrapped the shirt around his ribs. When he pulled it tight and tied it off, the corporal nearly passed out and would have collapsed to the ground if I hadn't been holding him.

Jamison put his head back against the rough wood wall. He took ragged, shallow breaths. "Whoo boy," he said when he finally regained his senses. "Now that was an absolute delight." Gunny handed him the canteen, and Jamison took a small sip.

"What are we going to do?" I asked Gunny. "I mean, look around. This camp is packed with prisoners. There aren't any supplies or food and barely any water. And men are dying right and left." I pointed to where the wounded lay. Many of them had been covered with sheets, too injured to survive their wounds. A Japanese guard with a machine gun was ordering prisoners to carry the dead men away. Off in the distance, other guards had captives digging graves.

"I told ya, Tree. I don't know. I suspect they ain't all organized yet. Probably didn't expect to have this many of us make it this far. But both of ya listen to me. Right now they got all the power. So the plan is, we keep us a low profile. Once Jams is back on his feet, we'll take turns standin' in the water line and keepin' the canteen filled. Until then me and Tree'll be swappin' turns. We'll share water until they issue us mess kits or rations or somethin'. Right now, I think we all should just stay here and get some rest."

Gunny and I sat down on either side of Jamison. The sun was moving through the sky and twilight was coming. There were men everywhere. Barracks were packed full to bursting, and any piece of open ground outside was occupied. Before long the humidity was pressing down on us again, and the heat was unbearable. But we were all exhausted and let ourselves doze.

A few hours later I jerked awake. It was dark now, and the moon was just above the horizon in the east. My muscles ached and I was stiff as a statue. I touched my jaw with my fingers. The swelling had gone down, but it still throbbed. I had to stand and work out some of the soreness. With a grunt I pulled myself up. Gunny and Jamison were still sleeping, and I made sure not to disturb them.

Slowly, I shuffled through the camp. What I saw was an army, thousands of men in various stages of distress. Rations and supplies had already been limited before we surrendered. At that point men were already starving. The Imperial Japanese Navy Air Service had control of the skies, so there were no supply drops. Some of the Filipino scouts had gone hunting and fishing for strange creatures that I didn't really want to think about but ate anyway.

The longer we held out, the worse it got. Then had come the march. Everyone had suffered, and many had died. Still more were dying now. As I walked I noticed the hundreds if not thousands of members of the Filipino Regular Army who remained in the camp. They were poorly trained, underequipped, and unreliable; some of them had slipped away into the jungle when the invasion began. I couldn't really blame them. Many were drafted right out of the cities and villages. Given little training and poor weapons, they gave up and deserted before things got noisy. I'll bet they never figured they'd end up here.

But the Filipino scouts who'd been assigned to work under our American forces were a different story. They were some of the toughest men I'd ever met. They stuck with us and fought hard. All of them knew the jungle and how to survive in it. And I believe they hated the Japanese as much as the Japanese hated Americans. The scouts were fierce and loyal and were determined to stay with their American allies. These seasoned warriors huddled together and glared at the guards with hatred in their eyes.

As I walked the compound, it buoyed my spirits to know that some of them had not only survived but also stuck with us. I was glad they had made it this far, but couldn't help wondering what horrors captivity might bring for them.

I hobbled about and discovered that it was not only American soldiers and Marines or Filipino scouts in the camp. There were British, Dutch, and Australian forces as well. Most of them tended to group together, and I supposed that made sense. When things got horrible, people tended to seek out their own countrymen, I guessed.

As I passed by a barracks full of Australians, I saw a Japanese guard beating an Australian who knelt on the ground before him. The Japanese guard was a small man—the Aussie looked like a giant by comparison, even on his knees. The guard held a thick wooden stick, and with a two-handed swing he clubbed the Australian in the back.

"Hah!" the man shouted as the blow landed.

"That's right, mate!" one of the men inside the barracks shouted. "You can take it, Marty! Tell him to take another crack!"

The guard swung again, and the club connected with a sickening thud on the big Australian's shoulders.

"Nothing! Didn't feel a thing! Was that a fly just landed on me back by any chance? You're gonna have to swing harder than that to lay a mark on this thick hide, mate!" the man shouted.

I was transfixed. The blows had to hurt. But the Australian was refusing to give the guard the slightest glimmer of satisfaction. He swung again. Another blow landed, and this time the Australians in the barracks cheered, "You show him, Marty!" The man—apparently named Marty—laughed from his knees.

The guard was confused. He stared at the men in the barracks, puzzled and angry. He shouted at them in Japanese, but they just kept laughing.

I smiled. This time the guard swung so hard the club broke on the Australian's broad back. Welts had opened on Marty's skin and he was bleeding, but he refused to show pain. This brought cries and shouts of delight from the men in the barracks. They all hooted.

"Attaboy, Marty," one of them said. "Show him what an Aussie's made of."

"Tougher stuff than that puny guard, Willy," another one of them shouted. That brought a round of uproarious laughter from the men in the barracks. It also enraged the guard. He tossed away the broken club. Pulling a small sword from his belt, he shouted again, grabbing Marty by the hair. He raised the sword over his head.

"No!" I shouted. The guard and the Aussie were only a few feet away. My muscles were still stiff, but I charged forward and tackled the guard, the two of us tumbling into the dirt. The Australians gave a shout and catapulted out of the barracks. It only took seconds before I lost track of what was happening. All I could see were legs and feet. I was too weak to hold off the guard for long, and the man flipped me over and sat astride my chest. He punched me twice in the face before two of the Australians pulled him off, the two of them twisting the man into the dirt and kicking and hitting him repeatedly.

There was shouting and chaos and more punches as other guards rushed in. Then everyone froze when several pistol shots rang out. I looked up from the ground to see Major Sato marching toward us.

"Enough!" he shouted. "Enough!" He issued several commands in Japanese and the guards grabbed the Australians, shoving them back into the barracks. I rolled over and tried rising to my feet, but I was in pain and it was slow going. Someone grabbed me and roughly jerked me to my feet.

I found myself face-to-face with Scarface. The jagged, lined mug and crooked teeth smiled at me, and I thought right then that I had never seen anything look so evil.

The last thing I remembered was something hard hitting me in the back of the head.

CHAPTER TWELVE

NEW FRIENDS

When I came to, I was lying on my side, curled up in a fetal position and completely disoriented. Something was terribly wrong. I tried sitting up, but I banged my head on something metal and collapsed with a groan. The pain in my legs and lower back was all-consuming. I tried to straighten out, but something was in my way. One of my eyes was swollen shut, but when I opened the other one I discovered I was inside some type of cage.

Slowly I remembered the Australian about to be stabbed by the Japanese guard and then not much after that. That seemed to be happening to me regularly. I saw dirt on the ground beneath me and could feel the sun above. I must have been unconscious for quite a while. When I'd left Gunny and Jamison to explore the camp it had been dark.

As hard as I tried, I couldn't stop the tears from coming. I knew I shouldn't cry. Gunny's words still rang in my ears. *Dig down deep.* But everything seemed hopeless. At that moment I was certain I couldn't go on living. It was the most miserable I'd ever been. Thoughts cascaded through my head like ocean waves. I wished I'd died fighting. Or that I was back home in Duluth, even if it meant taking another thrashing from Pa every night. His beatings were nothing compared to this. How could I have been so stupid?

When I'd cried myself out, I slowly raised my head a few inches and tried to get a sense of where I was. The cage sat next to the fence on the very edge of the camp. Twisting my head to the left, I spotted three guards about twenty yards away. They were leaning against the fence smoking cigarettes and chatting, none of them paying me any attention. I wondered where Gunny and Jams were and if they were looking for me.

All day I was stuck in that position. I thought if I didn't get a drink of water and straighten my legs soon I might go insane. I was reduced to licking some of the sweat off my wrist. Before long I was so dehydrated I wasn't even sweating anymore.

I dozed off and on. Twilight arrived, and two of the guards took off, leaving a single guard alone by the fence. I had no idea where the other two had gone, but the remaining guard acted like I wasn't even there.

"Hey!" I shouted at the guard. "I need some water! Let me out of here!"

The guard glanced over at me but ignored my plea.

"Let me out! Let me out!" I shouted over and over. Finally the guard sighed and strolled over to the cage. He stuck his rifle butt through one of the openings between the bars and poked me hard in the stomach. Then he spun on his heel and returned to his spot.

I lay there not knowing what else to do. I finally gave up even trying to be comfortable and drifted into restless sleep.

"Hey, Yank!" a quiet voice whispered from out of the darkness. I jerked awake, startled.

"Who's there?" I asked.

"Shh. Quiet, mate. Don't want to wake the guard, now do we?" the voice said with a thick Australian accent.

I peered into the darkness but saw no one. "Who are you?"

"Name is Wilson. But all me mates call me Willy."

"What do you want?"

"Me and a couple of the boys here have come to get you out," Willy said.

"What? You can't do that. They'll kill you if you try to escape," I said.

"Oh, we ain't escaping," Willy whispered. "Me and my mates is right bloody grateful to you for stepping in and saving Marty like you did. What's your name, Yank?"

"I didn't . . . Forrest. My name is Henry Forrest," I stammered, "but everybody calls me Tree." The disorientation and confusion were slowly overwhelming me. It made me wonder for a moment if the voices were all in my head. Was I hallucinating?

"Well, Mr. Tree Forrest, we're Australians from the 2nd AIF. We owe you for saving Marty. And a debt is a debt. I'm with two buddies, Smitty and Davis. We're gonna get you out of here."

"But . . . Willy . . . suppose you get me out? Won't the Japanese be awful upset if they find an empty cage when the sun comes up?"

"Ah. Here's the beauty of the plan, Henry. It won't be empty. Smitty here, he's about your size, and he got himself roughed up pretty good in that melee you started by knocking that guard on his tiny Imperial Japanese Army butt. Smitty's face is all askew, just like yours. But otherwise he's in fine form. Smitty, tell the boy you're good to go," Willy said.

"I'm in good shape, Henry. A fair sight better than you, I'll wager. I'm right as rain, as you Yanks is fond of saying," Smitty said.

"And you see, that's the beauty of our plan. Smitty is gonna take your place. The emperor's boys can't tell one of us from the other. Same size, same hair color, same messed-up face. It'll be easy as a walkabout. So Davis here, he's going to pick the lock, seeing as before the war he was . . . Well, let's not worry about what he was before all the shooting started. And Smitty is going to climb in the cage and pretend to be you, and we'll get you back to your unit. Nobody will be none the wiser."

"I can't let anybody do that. You get caught and they'll kill you," I said. "Besides, there's a guard in the camp—Scarface—he knows me. We already had a couple of run-ins. He beat me good on the march here. For all I know, he helped put me in this cage. If he sees me walking free, he's gonna wonder. And he's a mean one. I watched him kill a man right in front of me. Poor Marine didn't even do a thing."

"Scarface?" Willy asked.

"He's got a long scar runs down the side of his face."

Willy quietly chuckled. "Ah. I suspect old Scarface wouldn't be happy if he knew about that nickname. I'll say this for you, Henry Forrest. You are one righteous Yank. Tougher than a dingo on a bone, I'll wager. But Smitty here is tough, too. Probably the orneriest bloke in our outfit. And it's been decided we owe you, for jumping in and saving Marty. They'll let Smitty out eventually. He's got some water and a little food spirited in hidden spots on his person. And if they don't let him free, we'll come break him out, like we're about to do you. He'll be fine. Let us help you. If this Scarface sees you, how's he gonna know it wasn't one of his Japanese mates that let you out?"

I didn't know what to say. I wanted out of the cage in the worst way. But I couldn't let another man take my punishment. It wasn't right. I had lied to enlist, but I still considered myself honor bound by the oath I'd sworn to the Marines. A Marine was supposed to fight the enemy. If you got caught, you were a prisoner, and that was that. It wasn't like you could tag someone and they could come in and take your spot.

As it turned out, the Aussies made the decision for me. I heard the hinges on the cage door squeak open.

"Henry," Smitty whispered. "I suspect it's going to be right painful when we lift you outta there, being all scrunched up and such. But you've gotta be quiet, so we don't alert our friend over there by the fence."

Two pairs of hands reached inside and lifted me out. I choked down an agonizing groan as the sudden movement sent jolts of pain up and down my spine. The two men lay me gently on the ground. Now that my good eye had adjusted, I could see them moving in the shadowy light. I watched as another man crawled inside the cage. The big man named Davis locked the crate again with a piece of wire.

"Smitty," Willy said, "we'll be keeping an eye on you. Stay strong now."

"No worries, Willy. Gives me a chance to catch some shut-eye. Forrest, far as I'm concerned, from this point on you're an Aussie through and through. You're one of us. Ain't a man in our unit won't step up for you, if you need it. Good luck, mate."

"Can you walk?" Willy asked me.

"I don't know. I'm no—" Before I could even finish answering, Davis plucked me off the ground like I was a pillow and carried me off into the darkness. I was amazed at the man's strength; it was my size that had gotten me into the Marines in the first place. I wondered if all Australians were this strong.

"You know where your unit is?" Willy asked as we kept to the shadows, stealing through the rows of barracks and avoiding the light from torches and patrolling Japanese guards.

“I didn’t have a unit left, really. All that’s left of the 15th Infantry is me and Gunny McAdams and Corporal Jamison. Last I saw them, Jams and Gunny were sleeping against a barracks wall somewhere in the middle of camp. But I have no idea where—”

“We’ll worry about that later. Right now we’ll take you to our barracks. We got a corpsman can check you over. And Marty wants to thank you. He’s right grateful.”

“You shouldn’t have saved me. It could get you executed.”

To my surprise, Willy laughed.

“Aw, heck, mate. Do you want to live forever?”

CHAPTER THIRTEEN

HEALING

I was treated like a movie star when we got back to the Australian barracks. Every single man came forward and shook my hand. Even though it made me wince. Finally, the big man they called Marty stepped out of the crowd.

He was one of the largest men I'd ever seen. His upper arms were the size of pumpkins, and his forearms were thick and roped with muscle. He had a towel around his neck and used it to dab sweat from his swollen, cut-up face. Curly black hair and a thick beard surrounded his head like a long-haired cat wrapped around a ball.

He stuck out a giant hand.

"Pleased to meet you, Henry. Name's Joe Martin. Sergeant in the 2nd AIF. I owe you my life. From now on, if you need me—if you need any of these men here for anything—all you gotta do is say the word."

"I didn't do anything, Sergeant Martin," I said.

"Bah," he answered. "That little wallaby would've killed me if you hadn't jumped on him the way you did.

So from now on, you need the help of anyone in the 2nd, it's yours. And call me Marty, why don't you."

I glanced around at the faces peering at him in the flickering light of the torches.

"Something on your mind, lad?" Marty asked.

"Yeah. What's a wallaby?" I asked.

For some reason the Australians found this uproariously funny. They all laughed and clapped each other on the back. It made me feel good, for the first time in a while.

Another man stepped out of the crowd. He was tall and blond, tending to the thin side. He wore a pair of glasses with round lenses.

"Name's Howard. I'm a medical corpsman. Let me take a look at you."

They led me to a corner of the barracks where there was a mat on the floor. A couple of the men helped me lie down, and I tried to groan as little as possible. All these men looked exceptionally tough. I really didn't want them thinking I was a weakling. Corpsman Howard knelt next to me.

"Tell me where you hurt the worst, mate," he said.

I didn't even know where to start, but gave him a rundown of my injuries. Someone handed me a canteen, and I drank from it greedily. I realized I was being a pig and stopped, handing it back. Howard pushed it back to me. "Drink up. We got more water." I nearly guzzled down the entire canteen in one gulp.

Howard looked at my good eye and gently pried open the one that was swollen shut. It hurt, but I only winced a little.

"I don't think you have a concussion. Your pupils look fine. The swelling will go down." He probed my ribs with his fingers and then looked at my left ankle, which was also swollen. "Riggsy, get me some cloth and tear it into strips. We'll wrap those ribs and your ankle. I think the ankle is sprained, not broken. And your ribs are bruised, but I don't feel any breaks. I'll say one thing for you, Yank, you can take a punch. That little guard was going at you like a croc on a tasty fish. You took everything he had to give and then some. Well done. Now you best try and rest. When's the last time you ate anything?" Howard asked.

"I don't remember. Since right before the surrender, I think. A few days ago," I said.

Howard looked at the Aussies clustered around the mat. "Somebody hit the stash and find him something to eat." A few minutes later half a mango appeared before me.

I couldn't help myself and wolfed it down, licking the juice from my fingers. Then I lay back down on the mat.

"You go ahead and sleep," said Howard. "In the morning we'll find your unit. Who should we look for?"

"Gunnery Sergeant Jack McAdams and Corporal Billy Jamison of the 15th Marine Infantry Battalion."

"Done," Howard said. "Now you rest."

And so I did. For the first time since the surrender I felt relatively safe. These men were not going to let anything bad happen to me. At least not tonight.

When I woke up Gunny was standing over me, and he looked madder than mad.

"Why good mornin', Private Forrest. Tell me, did ya enjoy yer stay here at the Philippine Waldorf Astoria?"

"I, uh . . ."

"Yer lucky I didn't wake you up with my official United States Marine Corps issue boot in your hind parts. What did I tell ya about keepin' out of trouble?" Gunny's eyes were ablaze. I squirmed, desperately wanting to be anywhere else.

I glanced around and saw Willy and Davis standing on the other side of the mat.

"Looks like we found your unit, mate," Willy said.

"Looks like it," I said, not entirely sure I was as pleased about it as I'd thought I'd be.

Willy stuck out his hand, and Gunny reluctantly shook it.

"Don't be too hard on the lad, Gunny, if you please. He's a right tough Yank, and he done saved the life of our first sergeant. The least we could do was give him a little aid and comfort," Willy said, smiling.

Gunny looked at Willy and let out a big sigh.

"Look. I appreciate y'all takin' care of my boy here. But Henry is . . . I'm sure you understand . . . You're a noncom, like me. He's one of my men. And he's special. I promised myself I'd keep him alive. Trouble is, he keeps gettin' himself messed up and makin' my job harder. And I ain't got eyes in the back of my head. I'm gonna have to lock the boy up if he keeps wanderin' off like a two-year-old. And as y'all may have noticed, he seems to have a talent for stickin' his nose into situations that don't require it."

Willy's face broke into a big grin. He nodded at Gunny in understanding.

"Well, Gunny, I can tell you this. So far we've found fifteen of us in this camp from the 2nd AIF. The roughest, toughest, fightingest outfit in the entire Australian military. And as of now, your Private Forrest is one of us. So no worries, mate. We'll help you keep an eye on old Henry here."

Gunny shook his head and looked at me. Frustration was written all over his face.

"I don't know how ya do it, Tree."

"I like how you call him Tree," Willy chuckled. "Fits him. He ain't quite as big as the Sarge or Davis here, but you seem to grow 'em tall in the US of A."

"Yeah," Gunny said. "But lookin' at the size of some of yer Australia boys, I'm thinkin' I might have to change his name to Shrub."

Willy laughed, and I felt better. I could tell Gunny was over being mad, at least for a while. And the Aussies were growing on him. I guess fighting men were the same everywhere.

"All right, Tree," Gunny said. "We gotta get ya on your feet and back to the barracks. You ready?"

Willy and Gunny took me by the hand and helped me to my feet. I felt a little better but was still pretty sore. My ribs had been wrapped, making it hard to breathe, but with the bandage tight around my ankle, I could stand, though it still hurt.

"You blokes got any food?" Willy asked.

"No. Our hosts ain't seen fit to come by with a room service menu yet," Gunny said.

"Davis, hit the stash. Get these boys somethin' to eat," Willy said.

Davis walked to the far corner of the barracks. The building was like ours, a three-sided hut. It offered little protection from the elements, and the open side made it easy for the guards to keep an eye on us. Glancing about to make sure no one was watching, Davis pried up one of the floorboards. Reaching beneath it, he removed another mango and a banana.

He replaced the floorboard and handed the fruit to Gunny. I could tell Gunny's mouth was watering. Holding the fruit, he looked at Willy with wonder on his face.

"How'd y'all get yer mitts on the fruit?" Gunny asked.

"There are ways. You just gotta outsneak the sneaking guards. We'll fill you in."

"I'll look forward to that," Gunny said. He squirreled the fruit away in his blouse.

"Ready, Tree?" he asked.

"I guess, Gunny."

We left the Aussies behind to a lot of shouts of good cheer and well-wishing. I felt better but still shambled along, unable to take a full stride without pain. My mood had improved dramatically since they had pulled me from the cage.

The cage.

"Gunny, we need to go check on the guy they traded me out for. He's still in that cage."

"No, we don't, Tree. We ain't goin' back there. One of them guards recognizes ya and it's a bayonet through yer gut. The Aussies got it covered."

"I gotta make sure the guy is okay. He took my place, for crying out loud."

"Tree, I'm tellin'—"

He never got to finish what he had to say. Because when we turned the corner to reach our barracks, there stood Scarface. He was holding his rifle at port arms.

And he didn't have a happy look on his face.

CHAPTER

FOURTEEN

CRUELTY

"Tree," Gunny whispered. "This host of ours has got it in for ya real bad. You let me do the yakkin', understand? No matter what happens to me, no matter how bad it gets, you stand your ground and stay out of it. Am I clear?"

"Gunny, I'm not gonna let—"

"Darn it, Tree, I'm gettin' sick of arguin'. I'm givin' ya a direct order."

I didn't say anything. Fear had overtaken me again. Even though I'd stood up to Scarface before, I knew I wasn't brave enough to face him now. No matter how many pep talks I got from Gunny, I'd always be afraid. Why did I think that running away would somehow instantly make me brave? Who did I think I was kidding?

Gunny was trying awfully hard to communicate with Scarface. He was making a walking motion with his fingers, and repeating *heisha*. Gunny had been in the Corps for ten years, and he'd picked up some Japanese words. *Heisha* was the Japanese word for barracks. Gunny was trying to explain to Scarface that we were on our way to the barracks.

But the guard wasn't paying attention. He was fixated on me. For a brief moment I wondered if he knew I was supposed to be in the cage. I had gone in unconscious. So it was quite possible that he had helped imprison me. And now he could be wondering how I got out.

"Heisha," Gunny said again. He took me by the arm and tried to step around the guard, as if we were on our way to the barracks. But Scarface had other ideas. He stepped in front of Gunny and gave him a hard shove backward with his rifle.

"Yameru!" he yelled.

"I don't know what you mean, you little—"

Gunny never got to finish, because Scarface drove the butt of his rifle hard into his stomach. Gunny went down, landing on his hands and knees in the dirt. He sucked in a huge gasping breath as he tried to recover from the blow.

"Stop it," I said and stepped forward.

"No! Tree! Dang it. You stand down. That's an order, ya dumb Devil Dog."

Slowly, Gunny climbed to his feet. "Heisha," he said again, pointing to the two of them. Scarface shouted something loudly in Japanese and reared back with his rifle. But this time Gunny was ready for him.

As the rifle whistled toward him, Gunny caught it by the stock. Scarface could not keep the surprise out of his eyes. Gunny's giant hands quickly twisted the rifle away from the guard and flipped it in the air. It landed a good ten yards away, skittering across the hard ground and kicking up dust.

A wave of emotions washed over the guard's face. In seconds he went from shock and surprise to anger and rage as his eyes grew to the size of melons. He produced a whistle from his pocket and blew three sharp blasts. Then he pulled a wooden club from the holder on his belt.

Gunny raised his hands. "Heisha," he said. "We go heisha."

Scarface answered by swinging the club. Gunny blocked it with his arm. There was a loud crack, and I couldn't tell if the club or Gunny's thick, muscled arm had broken. I couldn't let him suffer on my account. I took a step toward them.

"Stand down, Tree!" Gunny yelled. "Don't lift a finger. Understand?" Before I had a chance to do anything, three other guards rushed in. One held me at bay with his rifle while the other two helped club Gunny into submission. Gunny cursed them with each blow.

"Come on, you bunch of cowards! My little sister hits harder'n that!" He egged them on until finally one of the guards kicked him in the jaw and he fell into the dirt unconscious.

As the fight unfolded in front of me, I yelled at them to stop and tried to get past the guard with the rifle to come to Gunny's defense. The soldier yelled at me in a high-pitched voiced as he brandished the gun back and forth, countering every move I made.

"Gunny!" I shouted. "Get up! You got to get up!"

But Gunny remained motionless, curled up in the dirt, not moving. His face and arms were bleeding.

All I could do was stand by helplessly while Scarface and two of the guards dragged Gunny's unconscious body away.

"Where are you taking him?" I yelled at the rifle-wielding guard. The man wore glasses and a Japanese infantry uniform. All he did was jabber at me in rapid-fire Japanese. I didn't have a clue what he was saying.

"Heisha," he finally said, gesturing with his rifle. "Heisha! Heisha!" I took it to mean he wanted me to return to the barracks now. The three guards dragging Gunny's unconscious body had disappeared among the rows of tents and barracks. Where had they taken him?

"Heisha!" the guard said again, drawing me out of my temporary reverie. And this time he was serious—he slid back the rifle bolt, and I heard the distinctive sound of the cartridge clicking into the magazine.

"All right! All right!" I said as the guard prodded me toward the barracks. As we walked, the guard kept poking me in the back with the rifle to keep me moving. "Keep it up, you little toad," I muttered.

Something had come over me. Watching Gunny being beaten had woken me up. I remembered what he told me. *Do whatever it takes to survive.* I could hear Gunny's words echoing in my head over and over. *Dig deep.* I'd dig deep, all right. The next guard that laid a hand on one of my friends was going to get a quick lesson in what was what, if I had anything to say about it.

Finally we arrived at our barracks. The guard's parting gesture—a blow to the back with the rifle—sent me sprawling onto the floor. The prisoners who witnessed the move said nothing. None of them wanted to invite trouble.

Once the guard was gone, I slowly stood and picked my way through the prisoners lying on the floor until I found Jamison. Jams was still in bad shape, but his face looked better, and some of the cuts and bruises were healing. He was lying on his side, facing the wall.

"Jams," I said, gently shaking him. "Jams, wake up. We got a problem."

Jamison came awake with a scream. Like he was emerging from a horrible nightmare.

"What is it?" he sputtered. "Holy Moses, Tree. You scared the tar out of me. What's wrong?"

"It's Gunny," I said. "They took him."

"Slow down, Tree." Jamison winced as he sat up and leaned against the barracks wall. "Who took him? Where did they take him?"

"The guards. The one I call Scarface, who killed the pilot on the march. Gunny just tried to get him to let us pass, but he wouldn't. He started beating Gunny real bad, but Gunny ordered me not to interfere. Then some other guards came, and they knocked Gunny unconscious and dragged him off somewhere. I'm afraid they're gonna kill him, Jams. We've got to do something."

"Stop a second, Tree. I know yer upset. But slow down. Take a breath. You gotta think about our tactical situation here. We don't know where they're holding him. He could be tied to a post somewhere. Or I heard they've got guardhouses on the other side of camp. That'd be my bet. If Gunny's still alive, they'll wanna work 'em over real good. Teach him a lesson. Can't tell ya how much I hate the little skunks." Jamison went on with several more colorful descriptions of the Japanese guards. Then he paused and winced again as he tried to adjust his leg to a more comfortable position.

"But Tree, there's you and me. So far we ain't found nobody else in this camp from the 15th that even knows Gunny. Sully and the others seem like good guys, but I doubt they want to risk anything for somebody they don't know all that well. And look at me. I can't even walk. I don't know what else to do except hope and pray that Gunny makes it through. You've seen him, Tree. He's the toughest noncom in the Corps. The man is built like an oak stump. I don't think there's a soldier in the entire Imperial Japanese Army that could take him. Gunny ain't gonna give 'em no satisfaction."

"That's what I'm worried about," I said. "Gunny will just keep on goading them until they kill him."

"Tree, I ain't gonna lie to you. Not after all we've been through together. You may be right. Gunny is gonna die on his feet before he lives on his knees, that's a lead-pipe cinch. But if he does go out, he goes out believin' in what he done. I wish I could help. I really do. But the opposition army has done a number on me. I can barely stand up. I ain't no good to you or Gunny right now. And you know I'd be right beside ya if I thought we had a chance to help him. But right now, I think all we can do is wait, and hope and pray for the best."

I heard what Jams was saying and knew he was right. But the thought of Gunny being starved or tortured somewhere was more than I could take.

"Don't worry, Jams. I know you're hurt bad. And I know that Gunny means as much to you as he does me. But I gotta do something. I at least need to know where he is. Then I'll figure out what I can do to get him back. Maybe I can bribe a guard to help."

Jamison looked at me in disbelief. "Henry, I know you're upset. But have you looked around at our situation? We ain't exactly flush. What are you gonna bribe a guard with? Sweat?"

I thought a minute. All we had was the canteen and the ragged clothes on our backs. But I had an idea. I knew who might be able to help me find out where Gunny was. And even more important, they might be able to arrange a way to spring him free.

"You're right, Jams. I don't have anything worth trading. But I know some guys who do. And as it turns out, they seem to like helping me out."

"What are you talkin' about, Tree? You ain't makin' no sense," Jamison said.

"I made some friends while you were laid up. And something tells me they'll be more than happy to help."

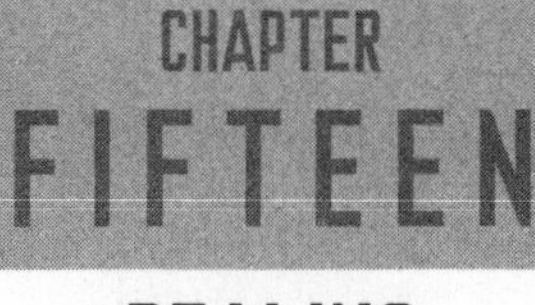

CHAPTER FIFTEEN

DEALING

"Slow down now, bloke," Sergeant Martin said. "Tell me again exactly what happened."

I was in the Aussie barracks, huddled in a corner with Sergeant Martin, Willy, and Davis. Davis stood with his gigantic arms crossed. Just the look on his face gave me the heebie-jeebies. Back home I used to read comic books like *Amazing Stories* and *Terrifying Tales*, and sometimes they had stories about robots from other planets. I loved reading them, and now Davis reminded me of one of those robots. I wasn't sure I'd heard Davis speak a single word. He seemed like a machine.

"They beat him up real bad, Sergeant Martin," I said. "Gunny is tough. He's like a piece of iron, and he's got a Marine's mind. But a man can only take so much. They wouldn't stop wailing on him, and then they dragged him off. I need to find out where they're keeping him, and see if there's a way to get him out."

Martin was quiet for a moment. Then he took a deep breath. "All right, Henry," he said. "First things first. We find out where he his."

He stood up, and I was again taken aback by the man's size.

"2nd! Listen up," Martin called. "We got us a Yank NCO who at this very moment is being horribly mistreated by our enemies. Every able-bodied man in the barracks scour the camp. Find out where they're keeping him. Move out."

Without hesitation, about a dozen men left the barracks and spread out.

"Nothing to do now but wait," Martin said.

"What happened to that guy Smitty, the one you put in the cage instead of me?" I asked.

A hand reached out and clapped me on the shoulder. I turned around and nearly jumped with joy to see Smitty's face smiling down at me.

"Hello, mate," Smitty said.

"Hey there!" I said, standing up. "Are you okay?"

Smitty stooped a little and moved slowly, but otherwise he looked to be in remarkably good shape.

"How did you get out?" I asked.

"Oh, it wasn't too bad," Smitty said. "Worst part was the blowies and bities swarming in at night and treating ole Smitty like he was a living, breathing chow line. Some guard let me out this morning. Just opened up the cage and walked away. So I made tracks back here right away afore he changed his mind. Corpsman Howard got me patched up and none the worse. Everything worked out. Just like we said."

"I'm glad you're all right," I said.

"Bah. Weren't nothing compared to what you did for Sergeant Martin there, laddie. You could have gotten yourself skewered like a shrimp. I only took a nap in a box. It's a fair trade."

"If you say so."

"I do. And don't you worry about Gunny. Sergeant Martin is the best animal in the entire AIF. We'll find your mate, and we'll come up with a way to get him out," Smitty said.

I must have had a look of complete confusion on my face.

"Something wrong, Henry?" Willy asked.

"No . . . I . . . just . . . I don't have any idea what Smitty just said," I confessed.

The Aussies laughed and laughed. All of them clapped me on the back.

"What he means is Sergeant Martin here is the best noncom in the 2nd Australian Imperial Force. When an Aussie is servin' with a right good sergeant like Marty here, you call 'em an animal. It's a compliment, is what it is. And Sergeant Martin here is a beaut. He'll figure out a way to get *your* animal back," Willy said.

"I feel like I should go out and search for Gunny, too," I said.

"Private, you don't answer to me," Sergeant Martin said. "But I think that's a bad idea. That bloke you call Scarface has a talent for showing up in the most unexpected places. And when he does, he takes a bloody instant dislike to you. You sit tight. My men are combing this camp right now. We've already got eyes and ears in a lot of places around here. We'll come up with his location in short order."

Part of me thought Sergeant Martin made a lot of sense. So far every time I'd run into Scarface all I'd done was get the daylights beaten out of me. Maybe sitting tight was a good idea. But the other part of me knew Gunny was out there and I should be doing something to get him back.

I stood up and paced back and forth.

"I don't know. Poor Gunny is out there suffering who knows what on account of me."

"Just by watching you, I can tell a lot about this Gunny of yours," Sergeant Martin said. "You're willing to risk your life to save him. That says a lot about a man."

"Your men were willing to do the same for you," I said.

"True. I try to treat my men well. Make sure they get trained. Get the supplies they need. Make fair decisions for them. But even doing all that don't always win you loyalty."

"They seem pretty loyal to you, Sergeant," I said.

"I suppose they are. But you got something different here, Henry. A different kind of loyalty, the rare kind. What makes you willing to die for this man?"

I was quiet for a moment. A hot breeze picked up and blew through the barracks. Flies buzzed around some of the sick and wounded. Sergeant Martin had eyes as blue as ice. He waited.

"Next to my grandfather, Gunny was maybe the first person in my life who never made me feel like I was a burden to them."

Sergeant Martin looked taken aback. He considered my words for a moment.

"What about your mum and pops?"

"My mother died when I was seven. My dad . . . he . . . changed after she died."

"Ah," Sergeant Martin said. He let the words sit for a moment.

"Let me guess," he said. "After your mum died, he started drinking. Got angry at the world. When he was most angry, he took it out on your hide. 'Cause you reminded him of her. So he tuned ya up a time or two. And your grandpops tried but was too old or couldn't control him. That about right?"

"Yes. Except it was more than a time or two. It got to be . . . a lot. How did you know?"

"Let's just say you're not the only one with that sad story to tell. So you didn't see any way out except signing up to fight?"

"Yes." For some reason, telling Sergeant Martin all this was making me feel lighter. Like I didn't have to carry everything any more. I looked out into the camp. Then Sergeant Martin shocked me back to reality.

"How old are you, Henry, fourteen? Fifteen?"

My head snapped around, and I looked at Sergeant Martin with wide eyes.

"Why would you say something like that? I'm . . . of course . . . I'm . . . I couldn't get in . . . I'm eighteen,"

I stuttered, wondering if I could sound any less convincing.

"Sure you are. And I'm the prime minister of Australia."

"No. It's true. I swear. I'm eighteen. The Corps wouldn't let me in if I was underage."

"Really? You didn't have a doctored-up piece a paper sayin' you was born a few years earlier? You're a good-sized bloke. Look older at first glance. But despite all that bruising and swelling, you got a baby face gives you straight away."

"No disrespect, Sergeant, but you're completely wrong."

"You don't need to lie to me, lad," Sergeant Martin said.

"I'm not."

"When Gunny came to get you, he was right mad. Yelling at you for risking your life. But every man here has risked his life. It didn't make any sense to me. Not at first. Then he said something about you being 'special,' but he couldn't say why. That got me wondering. Because excuse me for saying so, Henry, but you don't seem special in no particular way that I can see. Aside from the fact you're one brave Yank, saving my neck like you did. So I puzzled on it for a while. And that's it. Gunny knows, don't he? He's been protecting you the whole time."

I was quiet. Colonel Forsythe might have told Gunny or Jams they were shipping me out before the bombs started dropping. But if he had, Gunny'd never said anything about it to me.

From the very first day I met him, Gunny had looked out for me. He didn't let me out of any duties or anything. But he made me a Marine. He was always checking and double-checking my gear. Teaching me how to shoot better on the range. I could still hear his voice: *Aim small, miss small, Tree.* And whether he knew for sure that I was underage or just guessed it, he never said anything about it and treated me like an adult.

Now Sergeant Martin had figured out my secret, too.

"Look, kid, you go on pretending you are who you say you are. For all I know you could be fourteen or eighty-seven. I'll help you and go on helping you till it ain't physically possible for me to help no more. We're brothers, lad. Age don't matter."

So I told Sergeant Martin everything. When I got to the part about how the colonel had told me I was going home right as the bombs started dropping, Sergeant Martin laughed out loud.

"Sorry, mate," he said, laughing so hard he had to wipe tears from his eyes. "That has to be the worst case of bad luck I ever heard tell of."

"Yeah, well, the Japanese sunk the ship I was supposed to leave on," I said.

This brought another round of laughter from him.

"Lad, I have to say, that is rich," he said as he finally got himself under control. "Don't worry none, Henry, your secret is safe with me."

He was still chuckling when Willy came rushing back into the barracks, sweating and out of breath.

"Good news," he said, panting. "We know where your animal is, Henry."

CHAPTER SIXTEEN

RESCUE

"He's in one of the old officers' quarters on the north end of camp," Willy said, trying to catch his breath.

"How reliable is the intel, Willy?" Martin asked.

"As good as we can get," he answered. "I talked to an American private who's been working as an orderly in the compound over that way. When I described Gunny McAdams, he said he couldn't be sure but there was an American sergeant in one of the rooms they've been using to interrogate prisoners. When I described him, he said this had to be the same bloke. Said the bush rats had worked the poor lad over good. I asked him was they any other American sergeants in that compound he knew of, and he said no. Gotta be your animal, Henry."

I tried not to let my excitement get the best of me. Knowing where Gunny was and getting him out were two completely different things. And the truth of it was I had no idea how to rescue him. It wasn't like we could mount a frontal assault on the building.

Sergeant Martin rubbed his chin. Then his eyes lit up, and he grabbed Willy by the shoulders.

"How much we got in the stash?" Martin asked.

"Fifteen pounds and a few shillings, plus two packs of cigs the guards didn't get their hands on when they searched us," Willy answered.

"All right, here's what we're gonna do. You, Smitty, and Davis work out a schedule and watch that building for the rest of the day and into the evening. Find out how many guards they've got, when and how often they change watch, and if they're paying close attention to what they're doing. Take turns and switch it up often so nobody notices you watching. We don't need anybody guessing what we're up to."

"Right you are," Willy said, running off to find Davis and Smitty.

"What are you going to do?" I asked.

"I'm not quite sure yet," said Sergeant Martin. "Our information is limited and only halfway reliable. But for now, we'll wait until lights-out, and then we'll go and see what we can see. If we can sneak in and get Gunny out with a fair chance of not losing our heads—and I mean that literally, mate—we'll do that. If not, we'll see if we can bribe us a guard to look the other way."

"Do you think that'll work? From what I've seen, these guards are pretty mean."

"You're right about that, Henry. No Japanese soldier wants to be babysitting a bunch of surrendering allies. They all want to be out on the battlefield, dying a glorious death for their bloody emperor. So we're stuck with the worst soldiers that the Imperial Japanese Army has got. If they were any good at fighting, they'd be out actually doing it instead of guarding a bunch of dirty captives who they consider less than human."

"The *Bushido*," I said.

"You know about that, do you?"

"Yeah. Gunny explained it to me. No honor in surrender and all that."

"Exactly right. A Japanese soldier would rather commit suicide than surrender. But every army, all over this wide world of ours, has got its share of screwups and malcontents. Even the Japanese, who are always boasting about how tough and efficient they are. They think the absolute worst Japanese soldier is still ten times better than the very best Yank or Aussie or Brit. Which is a laugh—everybody knows the Brits, with all their boarding schools and afternoon teas, are a bunch of lightweights. Wouldn't last a day in the outback."

"I still don't understand. What's that got do with us?"

"What it does is make us lucky, Henry. Because maybe the guards we've got here *are* the dregs. They ain't happy at all to be here, and right now they're taking it out on all of us. But the commanders are a little smarter. They know these jokers they've got guarding us ain't gonna do 'em a lick of good on the battlefield. So they get assigned prison duty. Most of 'em are mean because while they may not know how to tie their shoes, they do know the reason they got assigned here is on account of them being screwups. Most of 'em are stupid. That's the reason why they're here in the first place. And them being stupid works to our advantage. They know there isn't any glory for them here. So why not line their pockets while they can? One of them blokes might even think he can collect enough hard coin to bribe somebody higher up the food chain. Get himself assigned somewhere else. That means if we can't sneak Gunny out, we might be able to bribe the guard to let us bring him back."

"Isn't that dangerous?"

Seargeant Martin looked at me with a bemused expression on his face.

"In case you hadn't noticed, our entire current situation is dangerous. We don't have many options. Nobody's coming to rescue us. This is about our only chance of saving Gunny. Saints be, you really are a young'n, aren't you?"

My cheeks colored as Sergeant Martin gave me a poke on the shoulder. "So what do we do now?" I asked.

Sergeant Martin lay his big body down on a mat on the barracks floor and yawned. "I got a feeling it's gonna be a long night. So if I were you, I'd try and get some shut-eye."

It was amazing how fast he fell asleep. Sleep was the last thing on my mind. I was a nervous wreck. But I found a space on the crowded barracks floor next to Sergeant Martin, stretched out, and closed my eyes. The next thing I knew Smitty was shaking me awake.

"It's time," he said as Sergeant Martin and I stood and stretched.

Willy gave us a quick briefing, but my mind was elsewhere. It was dark outside, and my stomach was rumbling. We'd been at the camp almost three days, and as far as I knew, the Japanese had yet to feed anyone. I'd even heard soldiers whispering that they were just going to let us starve. I couldn't believe that was true. But right now my stomach told me different.

"All right, listen up, blokes. Smitty and Willy will go first. Cut through the camp and come up on those officers' quarters from the east. Me, Davis, and Henry here will skirt the western fence. We'll meet up in the center of the last row of huts. It's open ground between them and the quarters, so we gotta see what the guards are up to first. Once we get there we'll decide who goes in. Davis, you'll definitely be on rescue duty—you're the only one of us strong enough to carry the bloke. Any questions?"

I had a million. But I didn't ask any of them. Sergeant Martin, Smitty, Willy, and Davis were good soldiers. And they were putting their lives on the line to help out somebody they barely knew, strictly on my say so. What kind of men did that?

Smitty and Willy left the barracks and disappeared from sight in seconds.

"All right, mates, let's go," Sergeant Martin said.

Making sure there were no guards about, we left the barracks and cut to our right around the building, heading for the western edge of camp. Davis took the lead, I followed, and Martin brought up the rear. I was amazed at how a big man like Davis could move as quietly as a cat. And Sergeant Martin, despite his injuries, made very little noise as we scurried along. Practically every step I took was a labor for me.

Davis stopped without warning and put up his right hand in a fist. We burrowed up against the side of one of the barracks, and a few seconds later two guards with rifles walked by, heading south, away from us. When they had disappeared into the darkness we took off again, finally reaching the last row of tents and barracks. Davis waited. He reminded me of a hunting dog. I imagined him sniffing the air to make sure there were no guards about. When he decided it was safe, he waved us forward, and we cut north toward the officers' quarters. Before long we reached the end of the barracks row and could see a cluster of small buildings near the camp's northernmost fence.

The night was nearly pitch-black. No fires were allowed after lights-out, and the Japanese quarters were at the other end of camp, near the kitchen. I had to strain to see anything.

"Do you suppose Willy and Smitty made it okay?" I whispered.

Davis whistled. It sounded like a birdcall, but not one I'd ever heard before. The same whistle came back from the other side of the camp a few seconds later. They'd made it.

We moved to meet in the center. Before long a couple of shadowy figures appeared.

"Who goes there?" Smitty whispered.

"My boot is gonna go there, Private, if you don't knock it off with the chatter," Martin whispered back. Smitty quietly chuckled.

"We've only seen one guard patrolling in front of the quarters so far," Willy reported, his voice barely audible. "If we time it right, me, Smitty, and Davis should be able to get inside without being seen. The hard part will be hustling Gunny back out. We gotta make sure he doesn't cry out. And we're for sure gonna need to help Davis carry him. As strong as he is, he won't be able to move as quickly with the extra load, and speed is our friend here."

In the shadows, I saw Davis shrug, as if carrying Gunny would be as easy as hoisting up a sack of barley. I'd still never heard him utter a word. When this was all over, I'd have to ask Smitty, Willy, or Sergeant Martin if he ever talked.

"All right," Sergeant Martin said. "Henry and I will stay here and keep watch. If anything looks funny, we'll give a whistle. That means you hunker down. Another whistle means the coast is clear. But if things turn batty, Willy, it's your call. You wait until it's safe and abort. Are we clear?"

"Abort," I interrupted. "But Gunny—"

Sergeant Martin put his hand up and stopped me. "Just because we might not get him tonight doesn't mean we ain't gonna get him. But we're going in blind. Something goes wrong, the main thing is to get out and live to fight another day. Everybody clear?"

No one raised any objections. We all watched silently as the guard moved past the building's entrance. When he was thirty yards away, Davis, Smitty, and Willy sprinted toward the door.

I never heard them move.

CHAPTER SEVENTEEN

NEAR MISS

The three men were invisible in the darkness. I tried to keep one eye on their general location and the other on the patrolling guard. He was approaching the end of the line of buildings, and before he turned around, I saw a sliver of light under the door of the officers' quarters flash on and off. The three of them had made it inside. So far, so good.

The heat and the humidity were oppressive, and I was sweating heavily. My heart was thundering like a thoroughbred on a racetrack. Blood roared in my ears, making it hard to hear anything around me. I wondered if I should have told Jams what we planned to do, but decided the fewer people who knew about our rescue mission the better.

Sergeant Martin squatted next to me in the darkness, still as a statue.

Suddenly, a thought hit me like a gut punch.

"Sergeant Martin," I whispered. "What if there are guards or doctors inside keeping an eye on Gunny? Willy, Smitty, and Davis could be walking right into a trap!"

Martin didn't move a muscle. "Nah," he finally said. "Don't worry, mate. Any prisoner inside that building is probably in the same shape as Gunny or worse. Much as it pains me to say it. They ain't gonna have any doctors in there because they ain't gonna treat anybody. And the Japanese won't waste resources keeping guards inside, since they don't think anyone will be escaping in their present condition. And if someone tries to make a run for it, they got a guard outside to either gun him down or sound the alarm."

It made sense. The Japanese still weren't organized yet. They'd have to be careful about how they allocated their details, since for all we knew there could be more captured troops coming in from other parts of Bataan. Although I didn't have a clue how they could fit any more men into this camp. I felt a little bit of relief. If we could avoid this one single guard, we could get Gunny out and hide him among the other prisoners of the camp. Then we could worry about getting him healed up.

The guard was on his way back toward us. He shambled by with his rifle perched on his shoulder, looking bored enough to fall asleep standing up.

When he'd gotten a dozen yards past the main door, it opened, and Smitty and Willy popped out without a sound. Next came Davis, with Gunny over his shoulders in a fireman's carry. Willy and Smitty kept their eyes on the guard. Davis, unbelievably, was moving across the ground at a trot. He was moving faster than I thought possible. Sergeant Martin and I watched helplessly, hoping they would make it across the darkened ground to us before the guard reached the end of his march.

It was going to be close.

"Come on, Davis, boy," Martin muttered. "You can make it. Hustle, laddie,"

They were twenty yards away, almost here.

Then everything went bad. Instead of going all the way to the edge of the hut, the guard turned around early. And despite his disinterest in his duty, he noticed movement in the shadows. He leveled his rifle in their direction and shouted, "Yameru!" The guard ran toward the four men, though he hadn't yet spotted me or Sergeant Martin waiting in the shadows.

Incredibly, Davis started running toward us, even with the added weight of Gunny across his shoulders.

"Willy, Smitty, lead him away!" Sergeant Martin called. "Don't get yourself shot. Henry, Davis, you're with me."

Smitty and Willy took off toward the east side of the camp. The guard stopped and hesitated, unsure what to do. Davis had reached us, with Gunny slung over his shoulders. We tried to press ourselves even further into the shadows.

The guard fired his rifle in the direction that Willy and Smitty had run. I cringed. If one of them was shot . . . I didn't have to wait long for my answer.

"Missed me!" I heard Willy shout. All of us breathed a sigh of relief. The guard took off in their direction and began blowing short, sharp blasts on a whistle. As if the gunshot wouldn't have roused every other guard anyway.

I was caught completely off guard when Davis spoke for the first time since I'd met him. "Willy says to tell you your animal is alive but unconscious. We didn't know how bad his injuries were, but we carried him out anyway. We best get him back to our barracks. Howard can check him out." He gave me a grim smile and started back the way we had come.

"What about Smitty and Willy?" I asked Sergeant Martin. "Shouldn't we try to help them?"

"Don't worry about them two. You ain't gonna find a slicker, more slippery pair than ole Smitty and Willy. If I know them, they're probably back at the barracks already wondering what took us so long. If they don't want to get caught, no guard's gonna catch them. Two of the cleverest blokes you'll ever find. They'll be fine. Now let's get going, before Davis leaves us in the dust and we get separated."

All around us the camp was coming alive. Guards were shouting, lights were turning on, and the sound of running feet was everywhere. Somehow Davis kept going, with Sergeant Martin and me following right behind.

We darted from dark space to dark space, shadow to shadow. Once we almost ran directly into a squad of Japanese guards. But Davis had a sixth sense about where we needed to go to avoid detection. I could barely keep up.

Finally, after weaving our way back and forth through the camp, we arrived back at the Aussie barracks. Davis carried Gunny inside and laid him on a mat. Gunny let out a groan, and though I knew he must have been in awful pain, it was the sweetest sound I'd ever heard. He was alive, and I had him back.

"Get a blanket!" Sergeant Martin ordered a few of his men. From out of the crowd of Aussies a tattered blanket appeared. Despite the heat, he covered Gunny up with it. He also took Gunny's dog tags and put them in his pocket.

"Why did you do that?" I asked.

"The Japanese know his name. If they see him in his dog tags, he's going right back. This way, if they search us, I might be able to convince them he's just another Aussie. There's a lot of men still beat up and recovering from the march. They can't tell us apart yet." He turned to his men. "Everyone hit the sack. Act like you've been sleeping and you don't know what all the fuss is about."

His men complied quickly. Everyone hit the floor and curled up or stretched out. Just then Smitty and Willy burst into the barracks.

"How close are they?" Martin demanded.

"Not very," Willy answered, catching his breath. "But I suspect they'll be here soon."

Sergeant Martin looked at me. "You think you can make it back to your barracks?"

"Yes, Sergeant," I said.

"Good. I think it's best you not be here when they arrive. Leave Gunny to us for now."

I knew he was probably right. It was hard to leave Gunny behind when we'd only just been reunited, but I trusted these men. I left their barracks and carefully avoided the guards on my way back. Everyone there was awake and wondering what all the commotion was about.

I said nothing as I tiptoed back to our corner and lay down on the mat next to a sleeping Jamison.

I had done it. Gunny was out. They couldn't hurt him anymore—at least not for now. And I had the Aussies to thank. I felt like I had scored a small victory.

Until the next morning, when everything fell apart.

CHAPTER EIGHTEEN

AWAKENING

At sunrise the camp was awakened by guards running through each barracks and tent, pulling every man able to stand outside to a large open area near the front gate. We were pushed and prodded until they finally had us formed into rough, staggered ranks. It took a while because there were a lot of us. Somehow I lost sight of Jams in all the commotion. By the time the guards had everyone in place it was already midmorning. The sun was relentless, and several men were already wobbling from the heat. A couple of them passed out.

When they regained consciousness, they were dragged forward and forced to their knees with their hands bound behind them. Even then, some were unable to remain upright and keeled over in the dirt.

I wondered what was happening. A few minutes later Major Sato appeared. He walked up and down the line of bound, kneeling prisoners, staring at them with contempt.

Guards surrounded us with their rifles at the ready. Major Sato studied us. I remembered what Sergeant Martin had said about the Imperial Japanese Army putting their worst soldiers in charge of the prison camps. Was Major Sato a horrible officer? Had he been given this command because he was bad at his job?

"Last night a rule was broken. A prisoner being held in our secure facility was removed without permission," Sato said.

"Can't be too secure if somebody got out," a tall, skinny Marine standing next to me said under his breath.

This brought snickers to those standing close enough to hear him.

Major Sato went on. "All of you were given a very clear explanation of the rules. Now someone has chosen to violate them. If those responsible come forward, there will be no repercussions. If not . . . we will have to resort to extreme measures. You have one minute to comply."

Without drawing attention to myself, I glanced around, looking for any of the Aussies. But the crowd was too dense, and I couldn't see them. The seconds ticked by. Major Sato looked at his watch.

"Very well," he said. He drew the samurai sword he wore at his belt. Before anyone could react, he stepped forward and with a mighty swing decapitated the prisoner on the end of the line. The man's headless body folded into the dirt.

At first the crowd stood in stunned silence. Then the prisoners began to murmur, which gave way to shouts and curses. The din grew louder as their anger swelled. Three men rushed toward the major and received a bayonet in the stomach from the guards for their troubles.

Someone fired a rifle into the air, and finally the crowd quieted.

"A prisoner will be killed each minute until the perpetrators of this offense come forward," Major Sato said. I froze. If only Gunny or Jams were here to tell me what to do. Or even Sergeant Martin or Willy or Davis. There were plenty of prisoners for the Japanese to beat on. Why would they miss one? What difference did it make when many of us were already sick and likely to die anyway?

"Time is up," Major Sato said. He raised the sword and stepped toward the next prisoner, who flopped over on his side, trying to get away.

The crowd began to shout again, calling Major Sato all kinds of names.

Two guards lifted the unlucky man back up. He kicked at them, screaming and cursing. It took the guards a few moments, but they finally got him back on his knees. He wouldn't hold still, so one of the guards grabbed his hair, holding his head straight up. Then the major raised the sword.

"Stop!" I shouted as loud as I could over the noise. I forced my way through the crowd to get to the front. "Stop! I did it! It was me! Don't kill that man!" The prisoners parted, and I made my way to the front of the group to face Major Sato.

He glared at me, his sword still poised. I held up my hands. I wasn't sure if he would kill the man just for spite.

Finally he sheathed the sword. I tried very hard not to look at the body of the dead man lying in the dust. He was just a poor soul killed for no reason. How could anybody be filled with so much hatred? War was one thing. Politicians made wars, and soldiers fought them. A fair fight was a fair fight. But killing an innocent, defenseless human being was entirely different.

"You are the one?" Major Sato said to me.

"Yes, sir," I said.

"And you had help?" he asked.

"No. I snuck in by myself," I said.

"You, an American private, hobbled and injured, snuck into the guard shack and removed a prisoner all by yourself?"

"Yes, sir."

"How?"

"It wasn't hard. I just timed it so the guard wouldn't see me."

"And you carried the prisoner. By yourself?"

"Yes."

"I do not believe you."

"It's the truth."

"The guard reported seeing two figures running away. He shot at them but missed in the darkness."

"He must have seen somebody else. I'd run too if somebody was shooting at me."

"Where is the man you removed from our custody?"

"I don't know for certain. I snuck into one of the barracks. Most of the men in it were sick and injured, sleeping on the floor. I don't think anybody saw me. But it was dark. I left him there. I don't know where it was or where he is."

Major Sato sighed. "That might be the worst lie I have ever heard."

I shrugged. "Can't help if you don't believe me. It's the truth."

"Perhaps if I kill this man, you will tell me where the missing prisoner is and who helped you."

For a moment I saw Gunny's face in my mind. He was telling me to dig deep again. To stand up. I owed it to him to try.

"No, you won't."

"What?" Major Sato seemed startled. "Why would you think I would not?"

"You may think I'm lying. But you aren't going to kill anybody else. You already made your point about how tough you are. So you're going to take me instead."

"Take you?" Major Sato looked at me, confused.

"Yes, sir. You're going to take me to that guard shack and 'interrogate' me. Do whatever it is you need to do. Beat me. Starve me. That's how you'll set your example. Because you know I won't tell you anything more. Neither will any of the men behind me."

Major Sato looked puzzled. Why was he being vexed by a lowly American private? The question was practically written across his face.

"I could kill all of you. No one would care," he declared.

"I think a lot of people would care. We're going to start coming back. We'll be back on Guam and the Philippines within a year. So go ahead, kill all of us. The United States military isn't going to take kindly to you butchering defenseless POWs." I tried to remember the map that Gunny had looked at every night. If I could recall the names of islands and battles in the South Pacific, I might be able to bluff my way out of this. But news was hard to get even before the surrender. I didn't want to blurt out anything that the major knew was wrong.

"Your military?" Major Sato threw back his head and laughed.

"Yep. Our military. You got us good at Pearl Harbor, I'll give you that. But we've got men and factories and ships and tanks and bombs and fuel and food, and we'll just keep coming at you until you're all done. You went to Harvard. You know we outnumber you. And you know we won't stop. So I think your best option is to take me into that shack. Do what you have to do to prove that you're in charge. I hope I'll survive it. But if I don't, well, somebody once told me that nobody lives forever."

Major Sato stared at me. "All of you look at him," he shouted to the crowd. "This man is a coward and a liar. He will be taken for interrogation. We will break him. I would suggest that those who helped him step forward now. You will be spared."

An incredible thing happened. The crowd of prisoners surged forward. It alarmed the guards enough to make them raise their rifles.

"I helped." All of a sudden Sully was standing next to me. I couldn't believe it.

"Me, too," said Worthy. He hardly ever spoke, but his voice was loud and clear now.

"I was there," said Martinez, the Marine we'd helped carry on the march. He was still pretty beat up and he hardly made a convincing accomplice, but he shuffled forward until he flanked me. One by one the other men from our barracks followed suit.

Before long every prisoner was hollering, "I did it!" "Take me!" "I was the one." The rumble grew louder as hundreds of voices shouted out in defiance.

Major Sato's face grew as red as a stoplight. His eyes were wide and his breathing ragged.

"Take him," he growled, pointing at me.

Two guards grabbed my arms and led me toward the guard shacks. As they pulled me along, I pretended not to hear Sato's samurai sword whistling through the air behind me.

CHAPTER NINETEEN

DELUSION

Hours later, I stood inside the shack, beaten and bleeding, and I thought about my mother. Through all the torture and abuse, I'd done like Gunny said. I dug deep and endured it. Memories of her were the most pleasant ones I had, so I concentrated on them. I remembered her reading to me every night. How she made gingerbread at Christmas. When I was five she took me by train to Minneapolis. We walked all over the city, and she bought me a toy train to remember the trip.

She always insisted that I use proper speech. She'd spoken English with a slight Norwegian accent, and she would tell me, "Right or wrong, people will judge you by how you speak, Henry. You must do your reading and lessons and learn the right way to pronounce words and practice your vocabulary." I always tried to do what I could to please her.

I recalled how different my dad had been when she was alive. We were almost like a normal family. And I never thought about the car accident that had taken her.

That night everything changed, but I couldn't dwell on it. Only the happy memories would see me through now.

The Japanese were enthusiastic and inventive in their cruelty toward me. At first it was simple beatings. They used four-foot lengths of bamboo about an inch in diameter. They hit me in the stomach, the chest, back, sides, neck, and shoulders—everywhere except my legs and head, because they wanted me conscious and able to stand. A couple of times I passed out from the pain. When that happened I got buckets of water in the face until I was awake. Then the beatings started again.

Scarface volunteered to work me over when he found out it was me in the guardhouse. Pleasure danced in his eyes as he stood back and leered at me. He would take a swing, stepping into it with all his weight and force behind it, then stand back and smile at me, his crooked teeth and scar mocking me.

"Didn't eat your oatmeal this morning, did you, Scarface? I hardly felt that one," I said.

He'd stare at me with narrow eyes. As if he didn't understand. Then he'd wind up and take another whack.

"Now you're getting it, buddy. Maybe you need to warm up a little before you start. Do some calisthenics. Get good and stretched out."

My back talk drove him crazy. My hands were bound to a rafter over my head, giving him full access to my mid-section. He stepped into position and swung the bamboo repeatedly into my right side. I thought I would die, and I tried to bend away from each blow to lessen the impact. But after a while my strength failed and I couldn't move. So he just kept hitting me over and over.

Another bucket of water washed over my head. The water was actually a relief from the heat and the pain, but I kept that information to myself. I wondered where the water had come from and if it would make me sick. Knowing Scarface, he probably brought it from the latrine. I hung from the rafter while he worked me over until the rope made my wrists raw and my legs could not support my weight.

Scarface threw the bucket in the corner of the room and walked out, muttering to himself.

"You have yourself a real nice day now, Scarface," I sputtered.

I'm not sure how long I hung there. I drifted in and out of consciousness. Eventually someone jerked me awake. It was another guard—I called him Big Ears—who cut my hands loose. I fell to the ground.

He was having none of that. Big Ears pulled me to my feet. Then he dumped a can of dry rice on the floor. I had no idea what was happening. Was he going to make me eat rice off the floor? It turned out to be much worse than that. He hit me in the back of the legs with his bamboo club, and I crumpled to my knees. Landing on the rice kernels hurt more than I could possibly imagine. Big Ears poked at me with his stick until I was kneeling straight up on my knees. He tied my hands behind my back. Hundreds of rice kernels dug into my skin. I tried to sit back on my haunches to relieve some of the pressure, but he blasted me in the lower back with the bamboo. A few minutes later I collapsed backward again, and he hit me much harder this time. Apparently sitting back on my lower legs was not allowed. Kneeling straight up put all of my weight on my knees. And it was torture.

"Are we going to have a tea party?" I wheezed.

Big Ears was not the talker Scarface was. Whenever I started to waver and sink to my haunches, he would spring forward brandishing the big stick. I usually rose up before he could hit me.

"I don't suppose this hotel has a room service menu, does it? A fellow gets awful hungry enjoying all the activities at this resort," I asked. He said nothing. His face was frozen in a surly, impassive mask.

"If there is room service, I'd love a club sandwich and iced tea," I said, mostly trying to keep myself awake, and my focus off the pain. He just stared at me.

"No? How about some bread and water?"

Big Ears leaned in the corner watching me. Eventually he fell asleep. When he did I sat back on my haunches. It helped a little. But by then the grains of rice had burrowed into my skin like leeches. I tried to think of a way I could rise up and clear a space on the floor. If Big Ears didn't wake up, I could get the rice off my knees, sweep away a spot with my feet, and kneel on the floor. He'd be none the wiser.

I raised myself up, but with my hands bound behind me, and probably a dozen broken or bruised ribs, I couldn't get myself into the right position. When I tried to stand I let out a yelp of pain, and Big Ears jerked awake. I tried to recover, but I couldn't move fast enough, and he caught me.

"Sorry to wake you, Mr. Ears. I had a cramp," I said. He crossed the small space in a heartbeat and the bamboo cane whistled through the air, connecting with the top of my shoulder. There was no bearing that one. I crumpled to the ground, screaming. I was sure he'd broken my shoulder or my collarbone. I faded in and out as he jerked me back to my knees, then returned to the corner.

The sun told me that twilight would be here soon. I was starving, but there were worse things to worry about.

An announcement came over the camp's loudspeaker. I didn't know what was said, but with a glare Big Ears abruptly left the room. As soon as he did, I keeled over on my side. My knees nearly screamed in relief. But there was still rice all over the floor, and it dug into every part of me. I tried to move, to roll over or stand. But I couldn't. The damp floor had puffed up some of the rice kernels. I licked them off the floor like a dog. It was the first food I'd had in my stomach since the mango the Aussies had given me. I figured it wasn't going to be nearly enough. *I'll never leave this room alive*, I thought to myself.

But that night I got my first indication that the world wasn't finished with me yet.

CHAPTER TWENTY

CHARITY

It was pitch-black when the creaking door caused me to open my eyes. A Japanese guard walked in, and as my eyes adjusted to the darkness, I could barely see anything, except that he wasn't carrying a bamboo pole.

He knelt beside me, lit a candle, and stuck it to a small tin plate. In the pale light I could tell he was very young. Maybe a teenager. It didn't matter. His presence still frightened me. He reached into the bucket he carried, and I steeled myself for whatever he might pull out of it.

To my surprise it was a tin cup. He held it to my lips, and I gulped the water down. He gave me another, and that was gone just as quickly. "Slow down, Yank," he said in heavily accented English. "Too much too fast make you sick." He filled the cup again and set it to the side. From somewhere he produced a cloth, which he dipped in the water and used to wash off my face.

"Can't clean you up too much. Figure out," he said. I guessed he meant the other guards would notice that someone had tended to me. Which would probably make my treatment worse.

"It's all right," I said.

Heaven came next in the form of a banana, which he broke up into small bits and helped me eat. It felt like the best meal I ever had. I didn't care if I got sick. Bite after bite, I swallowed it like a snake swallowing a mouse.

He held up a piece of paper in the dim light. It was hard to read the writing in the flickering candlelight. But when I recognized the handwriting, my heart nearly leapt out of my chest.

Tree,

This is a guy whose name don't matter. He's been bribed to look after ya at night. Hold strong. Me and your Aussie pals is workin on a plan to get yer sorry butt out of there. They told me what ya did to get me out. And we's gonna have a long discussion about that when we get ya outta there and I guarantee ya, ya ain't gonna like it. Until then. You. Do. Not. Have. My. Permission. To. Die. If you do, I'll kill ya a second time. Be ready.

Gunny

I couldn't believe it. Gunny! Just the thought that he was okay made me feel better. I read it quickly one more time.

"Done?" the young kid asked.

I nodded, and he held the note over the candle flame until it began to burn. He dropped it on the floor and then blew away the ashes.

"Yank, you need sit up. Ribs gonna hurt. Don't make no noise. Lie down, get sick."

He was deceptively strong. Reaching under my arms, he lifted me up. I must have passed out, because I woke with a groan sitting in the corner of the room. He put his hand over my mouth.

"You make noise, they come. Beat you more. Sit up. Try to breathe." He brushed a few of the rice kernels off my chest and arms and gave me one more sip of water.

As quickly as he'd come, he was gone, closing the door behind him with a quiet click.

I sat in the dark, wondering what Gunny and the others were planning. It also made me wonder how long I'd been in here. We'd taken Gunny a few days after we arrived. But with all the beatings and passing out, I had no idea how long they'd held me.

It must have been a while, because the note sounded exactly like the old Gunny. I must have spent enough time in here for him to heal up. And he was working on a plan. The thought of it gave me hope. For the first time since I entered this room, it felt like I could make it through this.

The kid had told me to breathe. I figured the guards had broken nearly all of my ribs. But I'd try to follow his advice.

I took a deep breath and felt like someone had shoved a red-hot steel rod down my throat and into my lungs. My mother taught me to never curse, but I couldn't help it. I whispered a long string of words so foul she'd have washed my mouth out with soap. I didn't want to attract attention. I could hear a prisoner in another room being beaten. He was begging and pleading for them to stop. The poor man made the most awful sounds; they pierced me right to the center of my soul. I wasn't going to draw attention to myself and get the same. But I was going to breathe no matter how much it hurt.

Off and on all night long, I practiced taking deep breaths. I lost consciousness from the pain a few times, but whenever I came too, I kept breathing deep until I grew too tired and fell asleep, my head hitting my chest.

The opening door woke me. Scarface walked inside, smiling and holding his length of bamboo in one hand. He looked well rested and refreshed. He also carried a length of rope over his shoulder.

"Good morning, sunshine!" I said, in the most cheerful way I could.

He didn't say anything and, pulling me roughly to my feet, cut the cords binding my hands. I rubbed my right wrist, which was raw, but he smacked my hand. Hard.

"Yameru!" he yelled. I'd learned that meant stop.

With my hands in front of me, he bound them once again with the rope and jerked me to the center of the room. He tossed the end of the rope over the rafter. It was then that I decided to do something supremely stupid.

Scarface turned around to face me, and as he was about to pull on the rope that would raise my hands, I kicked him hard in the groin. His eyes widened in surprise, and he sank to his knees. My knee shot upward like a snake and connected with the point of his chin. He groaned and fell over backward. The pain in my ribs after all that activity made me nearly collapse.

He'd leaned his bamboo club against the wall. Big mistake. I picked it up with my bound hands and went to work on him. I hit him in the stomach, the legs, and the ribs. But I had no strength behind the blows. I'd hurt him. But not like he'd hurt me.

When I swung the stick again, he caught it and jerked it away from me. He swung it hard, connecting with my knees. I went down, landing on my shoulder. The bamboo rained down on me. Scarface became a steaming ball of rage. He screamed what I could only assume were Japanese obscenities at me. His shouting brought the attention of more guards, who came rushing into the room. They joined him, their feet and fists pounding over my body. I slipped away into the darkness of unconsciousness.

* * *

A bucket of water brought me back to reality. I was trussed up, hanging from the rafter. That was all that was keeping me upright. My eyes were nearly swollen shut. But I knew there were men in the room.

A hand grabbed me by the cheeks, and I tried to focus. Finally I recognized . . . my father? What was he doing here? He should be in Minnesota. And why was he wearing a Japanese officer's uniform? He looked displeased.

"You," he said.

That was all. I was quiet a moment.

"Nice to see you again, Father," I finally gasped.

He squeezed my cheeks harder. It hurt, and I winced.

"You attacked one of my men," he said.

"Did I? Which one? I didn't know you had men, Dad." I was confused. I squinted, trying to bring my eyes into focus. For a moment my father became Major Sato. Then he became my father again. Was I hallucinating? Where was I?

"Do not trifle with me."

"That's a big word for you, Dad. Trifle. But don't worry. I wouldn't dream of it. As you can see, your *men* have done a fair job of attacking me."

"You will address me as Major!" he shouted.

"Now why would I do that? You aren't a Marine. I don't have to salute you, *Daddy*." I squinted again and grew more confused. My head was swirling with changing images. My father and Major Sato seemed to share the same body. Now Major Sato spoke.

"You are a prisoner. It is their job to punish you."

"So what you're saying is, if I'm all trussed up like this unable to defend myself, they'll do their worst. But they can't handle a fair fight?"

He released my cheek. My head waggled around, and I couldn't stay focused on him.

"Who are you?" he asked.

I finally managed a glance around the room. Big Ears and Scarface stood behind him. Scarface looked like he'd been roughed up a bit. That made me smile. Then things got hazy again. I heard the sound of laughter coming from my mouth.

"What is so funny?"

I looked up and my dad was back again. Standing there glaring at me like he always did.

"It's not my fault she died. You were wrong to treat me the way you did."

Major Sato whirled back into view. "Why are you laughing? What are you talking about?"

"Nothing."

He paced back and forth.

"Who are you?" he asked again. I tried to focus. His voice was weird. It sounded just like my father's. I shook my head, desperate to clear it.

"Private Henry Forrest, United States Marine Corps. Seria—"

"Enough!" he interrupted me. "I could have you executed for attacking a guard."

I pondered that for a moment. It was hard to concentrate on what he was saying.

"Nah. You won't." I tried to sound confident. He most certainly could.

"You are a vexatious man, Private Forrest."

"Vexatious. Now there is a five-dollar word for you."

"Do you know what it means?"

"Yeah. It means you don't understand me and I'm causing you trouble. Vexing you."

"Indeed. I think I will have you shot."

"I think you won't."

"And why is that?" Something clicked in me then. I squinted at the major. His face was fuzzy, and my dad kept peering out through his eyes. I was tired of it all. Sick of being beaten. Through with being blamed for things that weren't my fault and made to suffer for it. I heard Gunny's voice in my head. *Dig deep*. I heard Jams telling me being scared didn't make me a coward. I'd had enough. They could kill me. But I wasn't going to let them break me.

"You saw what happened when you brought me in here. Every prisoner tried to take my place. You shoot me and the camp will riot. You might put the riot down, but somewhere you've got a boss, and he's going to hear about it. And he's going to figure this Major Sato fellow is not up to running a prisoner of war camp. Next thing you know you'll be working at some other plum assignment, like counting all the coconuts on Luzon."

I was bluffing like I never had in my life. Sato could kill me right now if he wanted, and I couldn't stop him.

He sneered at me. "You could disappear. I could shoot you and throw you in a ditch. No one would know."

"See, that's where you don't get it. You think you got us beat. But we soldiers, sailors, and Marines haven't given up. General Wainwright surrendered—not us. And if I don't show up back in that camp soon, the men out there are going to get restless. You'll have more trouble on your hands than you can accommodate. You can only kill us. You can't defeat us."

"Any troublemakers will be gunned down like rabid dogs. The entire camp if necessary."

"Sure. Go ahead and kill us all. And you'll have a storm rain down on you like you can't imagine. You're already losing. You know it."

"Losing? Ha. You are a fool. Your military is weak. We will destroy it."

"You've got two choices. Turn me loose or kill me. Otherwise, I'm sick of listening to your gas."

Another bluff. And an insult to boot.

"You are a confident man. I will not shoot you. No, I think it will be more enjoyable to watch you remain here and die slowly." He turned on his heel and made to leave the room.

"Major?"

"Yes?" He turned around to face me.

I nodded toward Scarface. "Next time he lays a hand on me, I'll tear his arm off and beat him to death with it."

The major said nothing, and all of them left. Right then I understood something. The major was afraid. He'd been to America. In his heart he knew the Japanese were doomed. They'd picked the wrong enemy. We might be down now. But we wouldn't be down forever. And he was smart enough to understand that. Which made him indecisive. That was good for us now. But I had a feeling he wouldn't be around for long.

* * *

The Japanese left me hanging there, broken and bleeding. Soon, the blood from my hands and wrists was running down my arms. It was only a matter of time before I passed out again.

I woke with a start. The kid who'd been bribed to help me was back. He gave me more water. Pulling a small knife from his pocket, he cut my hands free. I nearly collapsed, but he held me up. He whistled quiet and low. The door opened and Gunny and Davis walked in.

"Tree, ain't ya ever learned to duck?" he whispered.

"Never felt better, Gunny," I muttered.

"Ya look like ya swallowed a hand grenade," he said. Davis, as usual, was silent as a stone.

"Better hurry, Yank," the kid said. "Follow."

Gunny and Davis grabbed my arms and wrapped them around their shoulders. Even with my swollen, slitted eyes, I could tell both men had lost weight. I tried hard to stifle my groans as they walked me out of the hut. It was dark outside.

"Where's the guard?" I asked.

"Davis took care of him," he said. I had no idea what that meant. Just as we stepped outside, doors opened to the remaining shacks, and Smitty, Willie, Sully, Worthy, and Sergeant Martin led other prisoners out of the guard shacks.

"What?"

"Never mind," Gunny said. "We got a plan."

PART FOUR

RECOVERY

1942–1944

CHAPTER TWENTY-ONE

HOPELESS

When I woke up the next morning, Gunny was standing over me. There was a man I didn't recognize beside him. He was short with dark hair and glasses. He had a friendly face, but like most of the other prisoners he looked pale and sickly.

"Mornin', Tree. Sleep well?" Gunny asked.

"Like a baby," I said. Which couldn't have been further from the truth. Every part of me ached. I tried to sit up and soon realized what a mistake that was. The room spun and my head hit the floor.

"Ouch," I said.

"I'd say," Gunny said. "Yer face looks like it wore out nine bodies. What did ya say to make them do that to ya in there?"

"Just expressed some opinions," I said.

"Well, it looks like they wasn't well received," Gunny said.

"Probably not. Still, they're clear on where I stand." I decided to change the subject. "How did you get me out? I saw the other prisoners leaving, too. Is the major going to stand for that?"

"The Aussies took care of it. They got some money together and bribed a couple of guards. They got substitutes taking your places, just like they did when ya was caged. We still all look alike to them guards, especially if we been roughed up a little. And the guards that worked ya over have been rotated over to new assignments. Another bribe to get the duty roster changed so the new guards ain't gonna know who's who. Here's the best part. Major Sato ain't in charge of the camp no more. He left a few days ago, and they brought in some other yahoo to take over. We got the kid who brought you the water keepin' an eye on everythin'. If things go south, he'll let us know. It's covered. No worries."

"Huh," I said, trying to figure it all out. I must have been gone longer than I'd thought. "It's awful risky, Gunny. If Scarface or one of those other guards comes back—"

Gunny held up his hand. "We ain't exactly livin' in a risk-free environment. We got you out. You stay in there, you die. Yer Aussie pals threatened to give me a thrashin' if I didn't go along with it. And seeing as how I figure I could only beat four or five of 'em at once, I agreed. We do what we gotta do. The Japanese is more worried about gettin' the camp organized than they are about yer sorry butt."

Gunny gestured toward the man standing next to him. "This here is Doc Sweeting. He was with the 17th Medical Corps. He's gonna check you out."

"Hello, Henry," Dr. Sweeting said.

"Howdy, Doc. Nice to meet you. I appreciate you taking a look at me, but I imagine you got a lot of other sick fellows to look after. Don't worry about tending to me," I said.

Gunny looked at the doctor. "Ya see what I mean? I call him Tree, but it ain't always 'cause he's as big as one. He's also as hardheaded as a twisted oak," Gunny said.

The doctor knelt next to me. "Let's take a look," he said.

He gently looked me over. I yelped each time he touched my ribs.

"Sorry," he said as he felt my forehead. "You've got broken ribs, at least three. Hard to tell exactly without X-rays. You'll need to try breathing as deeply as you can. And you need to walk a lot and sleep sitting up. You'll be at risk for pneumonia, and believe me there is nothing here to treat you with. I don't even have anything to wrap your ribs. I'm sorry," the doctor said. "You don't appear to have a fever, which means you probably don't have an infection yet. So at least there's that."

"Shoot, Doc," Gunny said. "Ain't yer fault. Besides, I got Jamison workin' on gettin' us supplies. In fact, I expect him back any minute."

"Jams?" I said. "How exactly will that happen? Last I saw him he was in worse shape than me."

"Well, that's the thing, Tree," Gunny said. "Old Jams healed up pretty well. An' like I tole ya, that boy is an operator. He's been workin' on gatherin' us up a stash of goodies."

"How is that possible?" I asked. "He couldn't even walk the other day."

"He's better now," Gunny said.

"How? How long was I in that hut?"

"Yer big mouth got y'all locked up in there for over two months," Gunny said.

I was stunned. Two months? Had I really survived in there that long? How had I lost track of that much time?

"You should be proud," Dr. Sweeting said. "Not many could survive what you did." He paused a moment. "Some haven't." The sadness in his voice was palpable. "I'm sorry I don't have anything to help you. I've asked the camp commandant for medicines and been denied. Some of the

Filipino scouts have told me about native plants that can treat disease and help with pain. But I haven't been able to get out on a work detail to gather any. Besides, the guards search everyone who comes back inside," he said.

"It's not your fault, Doc," I said.

There was a commotion at the front of the barracks, and the next thing I knew Jams was at my side. His face was still a little misshapen and swollen, and he limped along with a slight hitch in his gait. I couldn't believe how good it felt to see him.

"Tree!" he shouted. "You look like the dogs have had you under the porch for a while."

"As usual, I don't know what that means," I said. "But it's good to see you, too, Jams."

"It means it looks like you been chewed on for a spell. How you doing, kid?"

"Well, I'd really like to start working on my Lindy Hop right away. When the war is over I plan on going to Hollywood and putting Fred Astaire out of business. But truthfully, I don't feel much like dancing right now."

"Well, we'll see about that," Jams said. He was holding a burlap sack. He reached inside and pulled out a tiny bottle of aspirin and a bedsheet. "This oughta help."

"Where did you get this?" Dr. Sweeting asked.

"Let's just say I got my ways," Jams said. The smile on his face was like a beacon on a dark night. Being back with him and Gunny had me feeling better already. And the fact they had healed up and were acting like their old selves lifted my spirits.

The doctor wasted no time. He had Gunny rip the sheet into strips. Then he handed me his canteen and gave me four of the aspirin.

"I wish I had something stronger for the pain," the doctor said. "But these should help a little."

Gunny had several pieces of the cloth torn and ready.

"Help me lift him up," Doc told him.

Gunny and Jams each took an arm and raised me to a sitting position. It was agonizing.

"You need to breathe in deeply and hold it as long as you can," Doc said.

I took a breath and his hands moved like lightning, wrapping strips around my chest and ribs. It was only a few seconds until I had to let the air out.

"Again," he said.

We repeated until I was completely wrapped. When I let out my breath it hurt, but my ribs were wrapped tight. I hoped this worked, because it sure was uncomfortable.

"Let's get him on his feet," Doc said.

Having them lift me to my feet felt like someone dropped a locomotive on my head. I moaned and tried not to cry, but tears formed in my eyes.

"Don't you worry none, Tree. It's all right. Sometimes pain is like a big old boil needs lancin'. Go ahead and let it out. All of us has felt what yer feelin' right now," Gunny said.

The doctor was calm and quietly encouraged me to take a step. And another. There were men clustered around the barracks, and Gunny hollered at them, "Make a hole! Wounded man comin' through."

Each step was a revelation in how many ways the human body could experience agony. But these men had risked their lives for me. Nothing was going to stop me. I walked to the end of the barracks. Then they turned me around, and I walked back.

I was surprised by the reaction of the other men. They started to clap, lightly at first, then more loudly. "Way to go, Forrest," one of them said. "You showed those little piles of dung what's what." There were cheers and whistles and attaboys.

"Quiet, ya knuckleheads," Gunny barked. "Y'all are gonna make him a target. Ya wanna help him, find some food, maybe somethin' for him to sit on." Gunny's voice was still as commanding as ever, and every man in the barracks jumped to work. By the time I finished another lap, Sully had found a crate for me to sit on. Worthy pushed a can of condensed milk into my hands. Gunny punched a hole in the top of it with his belt buckle. I'd never tasted anything so sweet.

Jams, Gunny, and the doctor watched me drink, and I could tell their mouths were watering. I held up the can. "I don't think I can drink all this. Why don't all of you have a swallow?" Gunny pushed it back at me.

"Negative, Private," he said. "Drink it down. Sooner we get ya back on yer feet, sooner ya can get yerself in trouble again."

"That's right, Tree," Jams said. "Besides, the military representatives of the Japanese Empire have seen fit to feed us a delicious ball of worm-infested rice every morning, so we're way ahead of you in the old food game."

Dr. Sweeting excused himself. "I've got other men I need to see. Henry, you need to try to walk the length of the barracks and back once every hour. Tomorrow, try walking around the outside of the building. Then go as far as you think you can, turn around, and come back. You're young and strong and I think your ribs will heal. Remember, you need to sleep sitting up for a while and keep breathing as deeply as you can. I don't want you to get pneumonia." He left us and headed off toward the south side of the camp.

I was tired and felt like sleeping. But I had questions about what had happened while I was in the hut. Gunny and Jams filled me in.

Turns out the Japanese were finally getting organized.

CHAPTER TWENTY-TWO

ENDLESS

"Each mornin' every able-bodied man has to turn out for what they call *Tenko*," said Jams. "Basically they count each barracks to make sure nobody escaped or died during the night. Dysentery, malaria, and beriberi are startin' to spread, so be careful what you drink and who you talk to."

"We get assigned to a work detail. It might be cuttin' wood, drivin' a truck to pick up somethin' they need—turns out your average Japanese soldier can't figure out how to drive an American truck—or workin' in the fields or rice paddies," Gunny said. "Trouble is the guards ain't good at countin', so *Tenko* takes nearly half the mornin'."

"Also, and this is real important, Tree, they got themselves a rule," Jams added. "A week ago, a group a sailors had a woodcuttin' detail out in the jungle. One of 'em got it in his head to escape. Rumor is there's guerillas fightin' up in the hills. Anyway, this sailor slips away, and when the guards count, they find they're one short. They look all over, can't find him, and realize he escaped. So to discourage that kind of thinkin' they executed the entire detail. All nine men beheaded in front of the whole camp. A couple a days later, they tracked down the poor sailor and shot him."

Jams was quiet a moment. Unfortunately I had no trouble believing it was true. Not from what I'd seen and experienced.

"Food ain't much," Gunny said. "We get maybe an ounce of rice in the morning and one at the end of the day. It's usually wormy, and the flies'll be on it faster than a hound on a bone if ya ain't careful and quick. Some of the prisoners working the fields manage to sneak in some vegetables, and the Filipino scouts will bring plants ya can eat. Jams is collectin' cigarettes, which are worth more than money now. We can trade 'em for canned goods and such. They got prisoners workin' in the kitchen who'll sometimes swipe food that's meant for the guards."

I winced when a jolt of pain from my ribs shot through me.

"What are we going to do now?" I asked.

"What do ya mean?" Gunny said. "We're gonna do what I told ya, Tree. Whatever we gotta do to survive. But the main thing has gotta be food. Keep yer eyes out all the time for anythin' edible."

"Is anybody working on a way to get out of here?" I asked.

Gunny snorted. "Ain't gonna be no big escape. That's a sure way to get yerself killed."

"But in basic training—"

"Stop right there," Gunny interrupted me. "Basic training means nothin' in this camp. Yeah, we're Marines. We're supposed to not help our enemies and make every attempt that can be made to escape. But I'm tellin' both of ya right now, whoever wrote that manual ain't ever been in a prison camp like this. Escapin' is a one-way ticket to a pine box. Except here ya don't even get no box. They just dump yer body in a muddy hole. Even if ya got outta camp, where ya gonna go? It ain't like we can hike to China."

I didn't know what to say. I'd hoped, somehow, when I got out of that hut that things would be different. But they weren't. In fact, they sounded worse.

"Buck up, kid. Your Aussie friends somehow got their hands on a radio and smuggled it into camp in pieces. They got some electronics whiz to put it all back together. And the news is that the US Navy kicked the ever lovin' starch out of the Japanese at Midway. Sunk a bunch of their ships and blew a whole passel of their planes right outta the sky. There's word they's headin' in our direction, one island at a time. Don't mention it to nobody. If they figure out we got us a radio, they'll tear the place apart looking for it, savvy?"

"I savvy, Gunny," I said.

"And another thing. Be careful who ya trust. Times like this a man gets desperate. Ain't no guarantee if ya go runnin' yer mouth off another prisoner won't sell ya out for an extra ounce of rice. Loose lips sink ships. Any news ya hear, keep it to yourself. Don't share with nobody ya don't trust to the bone."

Over the next few weeks, I slowly healed. My ribs ached less, and I could walk longer distances. Before long I got sent out on details with Gunny and Jams. The two of them covered for me wherever we were assigned. They had to, because whether it was cutting firewood or weeding fields, the Japanese had a quota for each man. If you didn't make your quota every day, you didn't get fed that night. If you made your quota, then they just raised it the next day. There was no way to win.

And the food. All we got was a little ounce of rice. Once in a while there would be a small crust of hard bread, too. The Japanese lived off rice, but what they fed us was awful. Most of the time it was worm-infested and undercooked, and as soon as they plopped it on your plate, the flies came out. You had to shoo them away and pick the worms out as quickly as you could so you could gulp it down. It drove Jams crazy.

Going through the chow line was when Jams was at his absolute best. When the cook would serve his rice he would go off on a long, creative, and expletive-filled rant. Only he never raised his voice or acted like he was upset. But oh how he could talk. Sometimes the Japanese cooks, even though they couldn't understand a word he said, would bow at him, and Jams would bow right back. They thought he was actually complimenting them on the food.

"Well, what do you know? Rice," he'd say. "Haven't had it in ages. Had myself quite a hankerin' for it. Course usually I don't eat it with worms, but what's a little extra protein? I'd like to thank you stupendous piles of horse dung for the luscious repast you've prepared for us this evenin'. It's truly going to help my back, which is nearly broken from workin' on your super important yet menial labor all day. Would you mind sharin' the wine list? I figure a joint like this has got quite a selection. What does His Holiness the Emperor drink? Red or white? You're just practically the most gracious hosts I could ever hope to meet. I can't wait to come back tomorrow for the pot roast and potatoes, you miserable sons of donkeys."

Jams was creative and never gave the same rant twice. And because he was such a talker by nature, the guards never caught on. I figured he better watch it in case one of them happened to know English. Then he'd get a beating. But it turned out to be good for morale. It got to be we could at least have a laugh, wondering what he'd come up with next.

As the weeks passed, life didn't get any easier. You worked every day from sunup to sundown. If you were sick, your barracks commander had to vouch for you, and the others on your detail had to cover your quota. Gunny was the ranking noncom in our little hatch. He worked hard to keep everyone's spirits up and us as healthy as possible. Jams was always there, working like a dog. His sense of humor kept everyone laughing a little bit. Even Worthy, who was always quiet, would crack a smile. Sully thought Jams was hilarious.

"I swear, Jams," he said one day. "You've gotta be the funniest guy I ever met. Here I am, starving and bone tired, not to mention thirsty. And you can still crack me up. When we get back to the States, we gotta get you to Hollywood.

You'll put Laurel and Hardy outta business. How do you do it?"

"It's a gift," Jams said. "Besides, we're gonna be the ones havin' the last laugh. The Japanese Empire don't get away with no sneak attack on Uncle Sam. So if agitatin' them entertains my brothers-in-arms, more's the better."

Something had changed in him. He was less nervous and twitchy. More focused. And Gunny was right, he was an operator. He traded for whatever he could and snuck in vegetables after a work detail, which he shared with everybody. And with malaria, beriberi, dysentery, and a host of other diseases running rampant through the camp, Jams became a master of the black market.

When Gunny came down with a case of malaria, Jams really shined. He took over the barracks and made sure Gunny was taken care of. We all took shifts staying awake while Gunny was delirious with fever. Jams worked his magic. He'd wander the camp, trading for food, aspirin, anything he could that might help.

The only treatment for malaria was quinine. There was none to be found. Gunny got sicker and sicker, burning up with fever and delirium. Then one day Jams came rushing into the barracks looking worried and proud at the same time.

"I talked my way into a poker game and won enough cash to trade for two doses of quinine. I hope it's enough." Jams was getting worried. Gunny had always seemed invincible. Seeing him weak and sick hit us all hard.

Soon his fever broke. Jams had managed to get just enough medicine to pull him through. Although there was a part of me that believed Gunny was just too strong-willed to die.

"I done told ya, Tree," Gunny said when he could finally talk again. "Ain't no way I'm gonna meet the Reaper on this miserable hunk a rock."

All of us got sick at one time or another. Dysentery was the worst. It gave you stomach cramps, fever, and diarrhea so bad you had to rush to the head at the drop of a hat. And as soon as you returned to the barracks you had to run right back. Doc did what he could. Jams worked his sources, but there was never enough medication to go around.

A couple of months later we lost Sully to malaria. Doc tried everything, and so did Jams. But he couldn't get his hand on any quinine this time. Sully had been a big man, but like all of us, he'd lost so much weight that Doc said he just couldn't fight it off. We were slowly being starved and had no strength to stop the diseases that stampeded through the camp. Gunny took Sully's death hard. He'd adopted everyone in the barracks as "his unit," and he couldn't bear the thought of losing a man. Worthy and Sully had been close, and with Sully gone, Worthy withdrew. Most of the time he sat huddled on his mat, staring off into space.

The rainy season started in April. The storms were relentless. But it did mean we could collect fresh water in our tin cups and fill our canteens. It helped some with keeping the sickness away, but the truth of it was it was still hot and miserable when it was raining. The air was so thick with humidity it felt like you were walking through gauze. When it stopped, steam rolled off the puddles of water. It was more a nuisance than a relief.

And the critters. Rats, mice, spiders, lice, snakes, and flies the Aussies called "bities" and "blowies" were everywhere. Out in the fields we'd cover ourselves with mud to keep them away, but somehow they still found their way through. And Doc said they helped spread the sickness, too. Jams had a particular rat that vexed him when it got into the stash of contraband he hid in the barracks. He immediately declared war.

"I swear by all that's holy, your little rat behind belongs to me," he said. It was early one morning when he woke up and found the rat had carried off some of his cigarettes and a pack of chewing gum he'd acquired. He set elaborate traps that never worked.

"Keep it up, rodent boy. I catch you, I'm gonna eat you and enjoy every bite."

Jams even tried moving his stash, but the rat always found it. One night we were playing cards, and it scurried across the barracks floor. Jams went berserk. He chased it back and forth trying his level best to stomp it to death, but it kept eluding him and finally disappeared under the floorboards.

"You're mine, varmint," he said, breathing hard from the exertion. "I'm gonna kill ya. So get your affairs in order and say goodbye to your little rat buddies. Because you are goin' down." Jams was a good Marine and a great friend. But he sure was a different sort of guy. He never did catch that rat.

The only thing that kept us going was the Aussie radio. We heard the Navy and Marines were coming. They were taking island after island from the Japanese. After a while you could tell the news was making its way to the guards and they were getting antsy about it. Every time we'd listen to a newscast and find out about another island taken, we'd silently applaud and gain a measure of hope. And the guards would get meaner.

That was how the days, the weeks, and the months passed. Sickness, rain, or burning heat, nothing to eat, and unbearable boredom. Until late 1944, when the Allied forces were getting too close and our Japanese friends made ready to move us off the Philippines. They had a particular destination in mind.

Japan.

PART FIVE

LIBERATION

1944–1945

CHAPTER TWENTY-THREE

AT SEA

"They're movin' us because MacArthur finally got off his hind end and started cleanin' up this mess," Gunny said. "And it's about time. I sure ain't gonna miss this place, but my instincts tell me our next post ain't gonna be no improvement."

We were standing on a dock in Manila Bay. A few days before, the Japanese had moved us here from Camp O'Donnell. Now they were loading prisoners into freighters and shipping them off to who knows where.

"Well, personally, I'm hopin' this next place at least has room service and a sauna. I didn't get near enough sweatin' done at Camp O and the steam'll do me good," Jams said. "I hear it opens the pores and helps clear up your complexion."

Gunny and I chuckled. "Jams, I swear yer one of the strangest fellas it's ever been my honor to know," Gunny said.

The sun was hot on our backs. If anyone looked at the hundreds of us standing there, they would assume someone was about to load a ship full of cadavers. Over two and a half years getting less than five hundred calories a day will do that to a man. It was nothing short of a miracle we had lived this long.

After another lengthy wait, they ordered us aboard a freighter. It wasn't a cruise ship, and they weren't about to let us lay out on the deck. They herded us belowdecks into the hold. We had to climb down on a ladder. Some of the men were so weak they couldn't make it. If a guard could reach them, they'd get a rifle butt to the face. Once Gunny, Jams, and I made it down, we tried helping or catching those who fell or were pushed. But we didn't have the strength to do much other than soften their fall.

One guy came tumbling down and crashed into the three of us. It was Worthy, and he was in bad shape. "Grab hold of him," Gunny said. The three of us could barely lift him, but we managed to stagger through the crowded cargo bay, Gunny barking at people to make way. We finally found a spot near the outer hull and set Worthy against it.

"Worthy! Worthy! Answer me, Marine," Gunny shouted.

Worthy didn't respond. Jams felt for a pulse. "He's barely alive."

Gunny took Worthy's face in his hands. "Come on, son. Ya gotta wake up now."

Worthy just sat there, his eyes closed, his breath ragged. We tried to get him to drink some water, but it just dribbled down his chin. Jams slammed his fist against the hull in frustration.

The hold had filled up. So many men were packed in you couldn't stand without touching the guy next to you, let alone think about sitting or lying down. And when you thought there was no possible way for another man to fit in the space, the Japanese pushed in another hundred or so. The stink was revolting. Men vomited from the stench.

Soon the engines groaned and we were underway. The freighter was old and slow, and the noise in the hold was unbearably loud. Men were alternately screaming, crying, moaning, and wailing. Fights broke out over the tiniest offenses.

When the Japanese lowered a water bucket, people went berserk. The water was gone in a heartbeat. Men fought over it, stealing it from each other. They screamed and clawed at each other's eyes. Punches were thrown. The entire hold descended into chaos.

Several of the officers hollered at the Japanese to lower down a barrel for us to relieve ourselves. The guards would just yell back in Japanese. Finally they figured out what we were asking for and complied, but that only created more chaos as men fought for the right to use it. And the stench grew worse.

The first night out we hit running seas, and the waves slammed us around. Sixteen men died that night. In the morning the Japanese pulled the bodies up by rope. The guards probably threw them overboard. At least the seas calmed in the daytime.

Later that afternoon, we lost Worthy. He just slipped away like a puff of smoke drifting off into the sky. One minute Gunny was sitting next to him, talking to him, imploring him to stay with us.

"Come on now," Gunny said. "Ya can do this, son. I know ya can do it." But Worthy just never woke up. Jams felt his pulse.

"He's gone, Gunny." Jams shook his head. "Ya did what ya could, Sarge. He just was too sick to—"

"Stow it, Jamison!" Gunny snapped at him. "For just once in yer life, stop talkin'." Gunny pulled Worthy's body to him, embracing him, and bowed his head. He took it hard when he lost a man. Tears leaked from his eyes. I'd never seen him act like this before. Gunny sat there a long time, with Worthy clutched in his arms.

"We gotta let him go," Jams finally said. Gunny glared at Jams, but his eyes finally softened and he nodded. We carried Worthy to the hatch. When the rope came down, we tied him off and the guards raised his body out of the hold. None of us talked for the rest of the day.

We had no idea how far we'd traveled or where we were going. There were POW camps all over—Korea, China, and lots of other territories the Japanese had conquered. The ship could be headed anywhere. Gunny, Jams, and I finally made it back to the outer wall of the hold and squeezed into a space where we could at least lean against something for support.

The second day, another eight men died. That night the boat rose and fell with the swells once again. Men grew seasick, but most of them had nothing to vomit up, myself included. Thirst became a worse enemy than hunger. The heat in the hold caused condensation to form on the inside of the hull. Men became so mad with thirst they started licking the walls, including Jams.

"Don't do that. It'll make ya sick," Gunny said.

"Can't help it, Gunny. Gotta have somethin' to drink," Jams replied. He was licking the wall like a dog licks a bug bite.

"I'm orderin' you to stop," Gunny said. "I don't want neither of ya gettin' sick."

Jams let out a laugh. "Sick? Really? Like I ain't sick already? And you think you're still in charge of me? You woulda died of malaria if it hadn't been for me. You don't give me orders no more, Gunny."

Gunny jerked him away from the wall. "Dad gum it, Jamison, you are still a Marine. You'll obey my orders, am I clear?"

This time Jams snorted. "Marine? I'm still a Marine? Are you serious? I ain't been a Marine since they gave us up on that stupid hunk of lava. And neither have you, Gunny. I hate to break it to ya, but we ain't Marines no more. We're walkin' corpses. Probably gonna die anyway. I ain't goin' thirsty."

Gunny grabbed hold of Jams and jerked him away from the wall.

"Jams, I said—"

He never got to finish, because Jamison hit him hard in the nose. Gunny nearly went down. "You son of a—" Gunny said.

I stepped between them. "Jams, Gunny. Stop it. Just stop it. Don't do this." I tried to push Jams against the wall, but he was wild with madness. His eyes were bloodshot and bugging out of his head.

"Turn me loose, Tree! Let me go or I swear I'll kill ya," he shouted.

"No, you won't, Jams. You don't mean it," I said.

"You don't know nothin', you dumb country hick. Let go of me or I swear I will choke you to death." He wiggled and squirmed, until finally Gunny stepped in and helped me pin him to the wall.

Jams let loose with a string of curses, calling both of us every name he could think of. Gunny spoke quietly, trying to calm him.

"It's okay, Jams. I understand. Let it out. Ain't nothin' a squared away Marine like Billy Jamison can't take. Let it go, boy. Ya been proppin' up me and Tree since this dung storm started. It's our turn to take care of you now. So just let 'er go, son."

Jams started sobbing. He cried for a long time. He just collapsed into Gunny's arms and bawled. Gunny patted his back like he was burping a baby.

"It's okay. It's gonna be all right, son. I swear. We're goin' to get out of this. You'll see. Before long—"

He never got to finish.

A giant explosion rocked the ship.

CHAPTER TWENTY-FOUR

SINKING

At first, no one understood what was happening. Gunny finally figured it out.

"We're under attack. Dang if we ain't under attack! Hang on, boys!"

According to the Geneva Convention, POW ships and medical transports were supposed to have big red crosses painted on the sides of the hull and across the deck. Of course the Japanese didn't do that because they had no interest in whether we lived or died. The Allied forces had no idea their soldiers were aboard this freighter, and so they were attacking it with everything they had.

Another bomb collided with the side of the ship and blew a hole in the port side. The freighter was already an old rust bucket—it wasn't built to survive the kind of damage inflicted by bombers.

Dozens of men were killed in the explosion, and the ship started taking on water.

A couple more bombs went off nearby. Misses, but they still rocked the freighter mightily.

"We gotta get our hind parts topside," Gunny said. "Hurry!"

He plowed through the crowd, with me and Jams at his heels. But every soldier in the hold had the same idea. We were all headed for the ladder. There were men clambering up it, while others pulled and pushed to take their spots. Meanwhile the hold was filling with water.

"Listen up!" Gunny barked. "One at a time!" He shoved a couple of men away from the ladder, and those already on it continued topside. Then he started sending guys up. As skinny and sickly as he was, Gunny still had a presence that made men listen to him.

One after the other, men climbed the ladder. As we waited, the water rose to our ankles, then our knees. Hundreds stood anxiously until it was their turn to climb.

"Let's go! Move! Move! Move!" Gunny hollered.

The order Gunny had put in place fell apart when another bomb hit the side of the ship. The freighter was not a cruiser or a battleship. It had no infrastructure to stand up to this kind of assault. With just a few posts to support the deck, it was made to haul cargo.

As the ship rent in two, the ladder became irrelevant. We were going into the water.

Gunny, Jams, and I hooked elbows. We didn't want to become separated.

"Hold on!" Gunny shouted.

The freighter split apart, and we were sucked into the swirling ocean waves. We could barely hold on to each other as the raging force of an angry sea washed over us. I took a deep breath and held it. The ship fell away from us, sinking like a stone, and we kicked upward toward the light.

We broke the surface, and it felt like we had entered Armageddon. The freighter was part of a convoy, and the sky was filled with American planes exacting a heavy toll on the other ships surrounding us. Fuel burned on the surface of the ocean. As I treaded water, my heart leapt at the sight of those planes with the stars on the wings wreaking havoc on the cruisers escorting the convoy.

"Look, Gunny!" I shouted over the noise. "They're here! They're finally here!"

"Yeah. That's great an' all, Tree," he said. "But let's focus. Ain't a one of those planes gonna land and pick us up. We gotta swim toward shore."

We'd been sailing along the coast, so land wasn't too far off. But I wasn't much of a swimmer. Not after growing up in Minnesota. Even with all the lakes. I dog-paddled after Gunny and Jams. We weren't going very fast. We were malnourished and weak, and had to stop every few yards to gasp for breath. As the waves battered us about, I could see several heads above the water, paddling toward shore like we were. There were not nearly as many as I knew had been in the hold. I said a silent prayer. What a horrible way for those men to die.

We kept pushing along, but the shore didn't seem to get much closer. The planes had sunk two more of the Japanese ships and zoomed off. They were probably running low on fuel and ammo. It was strange not to see Japanese aircraft in the skies, defending the convoy. Maybe our side really was winning. The glimmer of potential victory gave me a jolt of strength, and I paddled harder.

As we swam, I thought about what would happen when we got to shore. What would we do? Was there a chance the American pilots had spotted us and would send help?

A small Japanese cruiser that survived the attack came sailing into view. It looked like we wouldn't even make it to shore before they picked us up. But then we heard their engines stop. I heard what sounded like machine gun fire.

The ship was firing on the prisoners in the water. To the north of us, they swept through the crowd of swimmers, and the guns chewed men up.

"What the—" Gunny said.

Everyone around us started swimming for shore as fast as they could. But the ship had multiple guns, and we were all easy targets inside their field of fire. Bullets flew our way.

"Deep breath! Go under!" Gunny barked.

We sucked in air and plunged below the surface. Bullets spiraled into the water around us. Whenever they struck someone, red clouds of blood bloomed around them. Bodies flopped and danced as they were riddled with bullets. And when the bullets moved on, the dead men hung motionless in the water.

My lungs were ready to burst. When I couldn't take it any longer, I pushed toward the surface. Gunny grabbed my ankle. I tried to shake free, but somehow he held on to me. I looked down at him, and he shook his head. Bullets were still darting through the water like tiny sharks looking to feed. Dark spots swirled in my vision. After what felt like hours, Gunny let go of my foot and we kicked to the surface. I sucked in a huge, gasping breath.

Finally the shooting had stopped. But something was wrong.

"Gunny," I sputtered. "Where's Jams?"

We spun around, treading water and calling his name.

No answer.

"Where is he?"

"I don't know, Tree," he said. "Jams! Jams! Jamison!"

Still no answer.

A few yards away a familiar-looking figure floated facedown in the water. I kicked over to him and flipped the body over. It was Jamison.

"Jams!" I gave him a shake. He wasn't breathing, and his lips were turning blue. I turned his head to the side and pried open his mouth. Water poured out, and he coughed and groaned.

He'd been shot. Several times. In the shoulder and the side just below and to the right of his stomach.

"Gunny!"

A few moments later he paddled up to us. Gunny felt his neck.

"He's still alive, but barely. We gotta get him to shore."

We each hooked one of our arms under Jamison's shoulders and paddled as hard as we could. It was awkward and slow. He cried out as we pulled him through the water.

"Hang in there, Jams," Gunny said. "We'll get you patched up soon."

Finally our feet hit sand and we could walk. As gently as we could, we pulled Jams across the surf to the shore. A handful of men were already there, milling about. We had no idea where we were. Gunny shouted at them to help, and several dashed toward us. Somehow we managed to carry Jams farther up the shore and lay him down on the sand.

He looked worse. He was turning white, and his wounds were seeping blood.

"Put pressure on his shoulder," Gunny said. I pressed down, trying to staunch the bleeding. Gunny was looking at the wound in Jamison's gut. Blood gurgled out of it like water out of a backed-up drain. He twisted Jams over on his side to look at his back.

"Blast it! No exit wound. Bullet's still in him. Ain't no way to stop the bleedin'." Gunny pounded the sand in frustration. He sat back on his knees and took Jams by the hand.

"No, Gunny," I cried. "It can't be. Not Jams. He took care of us."

"I know he did, son. Now we gotta be there for him."

"No. No. You're wrong." I stopped putting pressure on Jamison's shoulder, which immediately started seeping blood again. With both hands I took hold of his face.

"Jams. Jams. It's me. Tree. You got to wake up. You can't die. You can't. Me and Gunny won't make it without you. Come on, buddy. Please wake up."

But he didn't.

He died right there in the sand. He had no last words. No message for us to give his family. No last wisecrack.

The friend who'd made me laugh through two years of torture died in my arms that day.

CHAPTER TWENTY-FIVE

RECAPTURED

A few hours later, small boats carrying Japanese soldiers came ashore. They climbed out with their rifles at the ready. Gunny and I sat in the sand next to Jamison's body. I couldn't hide the hatred in my eyes.

"Tree. I'm orderin' ya right now. Don't do it," Gunny said.

"What?" I said, my eyes never leaving the approaching soldiers with their rifles pointed at us. What were they afraid of? That we might throw a handful of sand in their eyes?

"I know what you're thinkin'. Ya wanna rush one of them, wrestle his rifle from him, and go down shootin'. Do that and they'll end us all."

"They killed Jams," I muttered.

"They did. It's what happens in war, son. Folks die. Ain't nobody sorrier than me that ole Jams is gone. But if Jams was here he'd tell ya the same thing. Don't get yourself killed on his account. You know it's true."

I didn't know how much more I could take. Gunny was always telling me to dig deep. How much deeper could I dig? There was nothing left in me.

"And get that thought of just givin' in outta yer mind."

"Leave me alone, Gunny."

"Listen to me, boy. You're a Marine until ya die or are officially discharged from the Unites States Marine Corps. Until then yer gonna listen an' obey. Understand?"

I didn't answer. Gunny wouldn't let it rest.

"Marine, do you understand me?"

"Yeah. I understand you. Loud and clear. And now I'm officially requesting you leave me alone."

Gunny knew how far to push things, so he turned his attention to the Japanese soldiers on the beach, studying them silently for several minutes. They had clustered in a group, and an officer was chattering away with his men. It was an animated discussion. My curiosity got the best of me.

"What do you think they're talking about?"

"I expect they're tryin' to decide whether to keep us or shoot us. You see them start raisin' them rifles, get ready to run."

They didn't shoot us. At that point, I think I would have preferred it. We had to leave poor Jams lying on the beach. We had nothing to dig a grave with, and they wouldn't have let us anyway. The Japanese were in a big hurry. They rounded us up, loaded us in their boats, and hauled us to another ship. It didn't take long. There were a lot less of us now.

A few days later we were in Japan. We landed in Tokyo Bay. As they marched us through the town of Chiba, the civilians watching the procession cursed at us. They were motley looking, and I suspect would have thrown rotten fruit if they had any. But I recognized the look. They were hungry. They were low on food as well.

In a strange way, I felt sorry for them. Yet I was also exhilarated. It gave me hope that the good old United States might actually be winning the war. If only I could listen for news on the Aussie's radio. But they got put on another ship. I never saw them again. Didn't even get a chance to tell them goodbye.

We were exhausted when we finally staggered into a camp not far from the city center. It was maybe two acres. The barracks were smaller than the ones at Camp O'Donnell, but they had bunk beds. And the weather was getting cooler. It would be winter soon. At least it wasn't hot.

Inside our barracks, Gunny and I claimed a bunk bed. I climbed up on top, since as Gunny pointed out, "Yer younger."

For dinner that night—and for the first time since we'd surrendered—we didn't have rice. They gave us a cup of boiled barley. It tasted like paste. I almost preferred the wormy rice.

The next day we were assigned to our new work detail. The Japanese were putting us to work at a steel mill belonging to Kawasaki Heavy Industries. The camp was close to the plant's entrance. My assignment was to shovel coal into a blast furnace, which melted iron ore. The molten ore flowed down a sluice and disappeared from view. It was hot and dirty work. I wore my T-shirt pulled over my nose to keep from breathing in coal dust.

Hot sparks would fly around from the burning coal. They landed on my skin and burned like a thousand fire ants crawling all over me. I brushed them off quickly, but any exposed skin on my body was pockmarked with burns in a matter of weeks.

I hadn't thought it possible, but the guards here were worse than any we'd seen so far. One day, after shoveling coal for two weeks, twelve hours a day, I passed out. Crumpled to the floor right there by the furnace. I came to with a guard I called Dr. Jekyll pounding on me with a wooden rod. It wasn't exactly an efficient way to bring someone back to consciousness. I finally climbed back to my feet. He got in my face and began yelling and screaming. I was woozy and wobbling on my feet. But I managed to roll my eyes at him, which got me another whack. I vowed I wouldn't give him the satisfaction of seeing the pain I was in or how much I'd come to hate the men who abused us. Losing Jams had been the last straw. Every night, I lay in my bunk and plotted elaborate revenge scenarios on the lot of them. But for now talking back was the only act of defiance I could muster. I'd think about Jams and wonder what kind of earful he'd give them. I could never come up with anything as good as I imagined he would say.

"One day I'm going to have the stick. And I'm going to enjoy testing it out on your hide. And by the way, if you have a toothbrush, you might want to use it at least once a week. Your breath smells like horse manure."

He had no idea what I was saying, so he shoved me. My shovel clattered to the floor, and my head spun when I bent to pick it up. I didn't want to, but I went back to work. What else could I do? At the end of the day I got another beating from Dr. Jekyll for not meeting my quota.

And that's how it went day after day, week after week. I had long since lost track of what day it was. I wasn't even sure of the year. All I knew was the weather had gotten cold, and of course the Japanese gave us only a few threadbare blankets. I didn't need warm clothing to shovel coal, but all of us men nearly froze every time we ventured outside and shivered in the barracks each evening.

"Gunny. I don't think I can go on," I said one night.

"That ain't true. Notice how all these Japanese is acting lately? Getting meaner, all nervous and jittery? That tells me things ain't goin' so well for the Japanese Empire. We don't ever see any Japanese planes fly over. I don't think they have many left. And they ain't got enough workforce or materials left to make new ones. I think they're gettin' their hind parts kicked by Uncle Sam."

No matter how hard I tried, I couldn't share his enthusiasm. I was exhausted. And the winter was brutal. Finally the Japanese figured out they couldn't have their workforce freezing to death, so some of us got pants. And they let us build small fires in the barracks at night in cutoff steel barrels. My pants burned up quick in the coal room. Before long they seemed more like a grass skirt, but I never got another pair.

That wasn't my biggest problem, though. Gunny was getting weaker. I started sharing some of my food with him. At first he wouldn't take it. But sometimes we'd just sit on his bunk with our cups of mush and he'd go into this trancelike state. When he did that, I'd scoop a spoonful of my food into his cup. He never noticed.

"Gunny. You need to eat up."

"Huh?" he'd murmur.

"I said you need to eat up. The grueled barley is especially good tonight."

"Oh. Yeah. Gotta keep up my strength." He'd finally wolf down his food.

The fact that Gunny might be losing his will bothered me almost as much as losing Jams. Gunny had been a pillar through this entire ordeal. Now he was quiet and stared off into space all the time.

The truth of it was all of us were feeling a lot like Gunny. We were turning into nothing more than walking skeletons. Each day of that long, cold winter was just a repetition of the day before.

Then spring arrived. That's when everything changed.

American warplanes began firebombing Tokyo.

We were going to win the war.

CHAPTER

TWENTY-SIX

THE BEGINNING

For forty-eight straight hours the US dropped incendiary bombs all over the city. The flames devastated Tokyo. The bombing was unrelenting. The planes were big bombers we'd never seen before. They dove in over the city and dropped their payloads. Seconds later huge fireballs would bloom all over town.

The carnage was almost inconceivable. I couldn't see it, but I knew tens of thousands of civilians were dying. The unmistakable smell of burning flesh wafted over the camp.

The bombing and burning continued until there wasn't a building higher than two stories for as far as we could see. The Japanese had no air support, only anti-aircraft guns. They managed to shoot down a few of the planes, but they couldn't keep up with the bombardment.

They kept us working in the steel mill. But before long, the blazes started heading our way. The prison camp was down to a skeleton crew of guards. The others had all been sent off to fight the fires. And the remaining guards paid little attention to us. We had the run of the camp. One of the guys snuck into a storage shed and found Red Cross boxes full of food, cigarettes, aspirin, decks of cards, and books to read. It looked like the guards had already gone through the boxes and took out what they wanted. So we decided the rest was fair game.

We cleaned out that shed and hid the goods. Everybody in the camp got at least one can of Spam. The first bite tasted like an angel was dancing on my tongue. We had to eat it slow. Some guys couldn't help themselves and wolfed it right down, which only meant it came right back up. Our systems couldn't handle all that protein at once. But by the end of the night, it was all gone. We buried the cans so the guards wouldn't find them.

The food and bombers seemed to snap Gunny out of his depression.

"Those have got to be the prettiest ugly planes I ever saw," he said as another flight of bombers swooped over Tokyo. It wasn't all elation, though. Every day the fire engulfing Tokyo burned, it grew closer to the mill. We could hear it creak and moan as the buildings around us collapsed. Finally, they shut the mill down. The next morning a bunch of trucks pulled up. The four remaining guards herded us into them. We guessed we'd gone about fifty miles before the trucks stopped in front of another work camp. They'd moved us to an iron mine closer to Nagasaki, and they wasted no time putting us to work.

"What do you suppose this place is, Gunny?"

"I reckon I don't know, Tree. I expect it's a big ole hole in the ground and they're gonna request we dig somethin' out of it."

Civilians ran the mine, with guards as backup muscle. And by any standard they were worse than the guards at the mill. By then the news of the death and destruction in Tokyo had reached them, and they took out their anger and desire for revenge on us.

They would make us stand at attention for hours until we passed out. Our food was cut back from nothing to half of nothing. Maybe some grains or raw rice. When we walked from the camp to the mine every morning, women and children would line up to throw stones and hit us with sticks as we walked by.

As the days turned into weeks, and the weeks turned into months, the bombings continued. If it wasn't for the sheer excitement of watching American planes pound the country into rubble, the monotony might have killed us. Somehow a guy in camp got hold of a can of white paint. At night he climbed up on the roof of one of the barracks and painted POW in big, white letters. It came in real handy one evening when a bomber appeared on the horizon. It started to dive toward the compound. All of us jumped up and down waving our arms and yelling as if the pilot of one of those big planes could hear us.

At the last second the pilot must have spotted the painted sign, because he pulled up, wagged his wings, and flew off. A day later another plane flew over. The bomb doors opened, and a bunch of packages with tiny parachutes attached to them floated down from the sky. The Japanese mine foremen and the guards tried to stop us from getting them, but there were too many of us and too few of them. Some of the men took beatings, but they couldn't stop all of us from getting our hands on the packages. We snatched them right out of the air, hustled through the camp, and hid the contents.

The boxes contained food and all kinds of supplies, like underwear and medicine. But the best part was the notes telling us to hold on, that help was on the way. There were also orders inside the boxes telling us not to take any chances. We were not to try to escape or overthrow the camps. The Japanese were on their last legs, and we should stay safe in our camps. They had identified the POW facilities and knew where we were. If we stayed in the camps, there was less chance we'd be injured or killed in a bombing run. They would continue regular supply drops. Those boxes were literal lifelines.

"I swear, Tree," Gunny said as we devoured a can of peaches. "I think ya've gained weight. Couple weeks ago, when ya turned sideways and stuck out your tongue ya looked like a zipper."

"You look better, too, Sarge."

The planes kept dropping packages, infuriating the Japanese. Beatings became more frequent and more vicious. I could understand that they were sore they were losing the war. But I'd had just about enough of them taking it out on us. So during a routine beating for something I wasn't even sure I'd done, I wrestled the pole away from a foreman and gave him a whipping, so he could see how it felt. The other foremen and two of the guards jumped into the fray and worked me over good. When they were done I could barely stand, but they ordered me down into the mine anyway.

The foremen had an office near the entrance to the mine. It had windows on all four sides. They sat in it all day monitoring the workers and counting the ore cars we pushed out of the tunnels. They had to be using the iron to manufacture weapons, but I couldn't understand why they were even bothering. Their capital city was in ruins. They didn't have enough planes or ships to wage war any longer. Why didn't they throw in the towel and surrender?

My job that day was on the dynamite detail. We'd drill holes in the wall, put in a stick of dynamite, and light the fuse. Then we'd run away like a stampeding herd of horses. The explosion would blow pieces of the ore out of the tunnel walls, and then we'd pick up the chunks and put them in the cart. I could barely move when I lit the fuse on my first stick. I couldn't run as fast as I needed to, and shrapnel from the explosion tore into my back and legs, knocking me to the ground. The pain was unbearable. I made it to my hands and knees and tried to stand up. I couldn't.

A guard shouted at me. I believe he was telling me to get back to work, and he kicked me in the ribs.

"I don't understand you. How'd you get that ugly face? I've seen cow dung prettier than you."

I know he didn't understand me, either, but I got another kick anyway.

I made it to my feet and staggered back down the tunnel. Then a thought hit me like a lightning bolt. The Japanese were losing the war. But despite the toll it was taking on their own people, they wouldn't give up. They were going to keep fighting until the Allied forces invaded and killed them all.

I decided then that despite our orders, I was going to fight back. I'd had enough. Done enough. Been beaten and starved enough. Watched my friends die enough. So I didn't care what kind of punishment I'd face. They could court-martial me if I survived the war. But that wouldn't stop me. From now on I was going to give as good as I got.

Fighting through the pain, it took me a long time to fill the cart. When I'd finally managed it, another prisoner came and pushed it toward the exit. The guard stood a bit farther down the tunnel, and he wasn't really paying attention. I positioned my body to block my hands from his line of vision, bent over the crate, and grabbed a stick of dynamite. I glanced over my shoulder, then took four more and stuffed them inside the waistband of my pants, pulling my shirt over them.

I didn't want to draw attention for not working, so I cut a long piece of the detonator cord and jammed it into a hole in the tunnel wall. But while I pretended to be readying to blast the rock, I cut another length of cord and stuffed it in my underwear.

Over the next few days, I managed to get my hands on tape and a small detonator. I smuggled everything back to camp and hid it in our barracks. When I had everything I needed, I waited until late one night when Gunny was asleep to put my plan into action. I taped the dynamite together and inserted the det cord. With the makeshift bomb in one hand and the detonator in the other, I snuck out of the barracks and made my way to the gate. Unsurprisingly, no one was guarding. There were so few guards at this point that they just kept it locked with a chain and padlock.

I walked like an old man, doubled over and shuffling along, until I reached the last row of barracks and the gate beyond. There was no one about. As quickly as I could I crossed to the wooden gate. It was only a little over six feet high. The pain and soreness I felt from all the beatings made climbing difficult, and I worried a guard might wander by and spot me, but no one did. Finally I was on the other side.

Once over, I headed straight for the mine entrance. The office was dark. I walked around behind it so no one from the camp could see me. There were a lot of rocks and detritus around the office, which was perfect for me—no one would ever notice where I was planting the bomb. I scratched out a hole in the dirt for the dynamite and inserted the det cord. Then I found a small pile of rocks about two hundred feet away. It was big enough to provide me cover. I covered the cord with dirt and rocks and left the detonator buried in the rock pile. Now I just had to wait for the perfect moment to put my plan into action.

We'll see who takes a beating now, I thought as I headed back to camp.

CHAPTER TWENTY-SEVEN
RELEASE

The next morning was gray and overcast. It started out like any other, but then something strange happened. We heard a big explosion to the east. Bigger than any we'd ever heard before. Despite how loud it was, it sounded far away. All of a sudden the guards and foremen got very agitated. They ordered us to work, but they were listening to a radio with real attention and horrified looks on their faces. They had removed their hats, and some of them were crying. Regardless, we still had to work.

Their strange behavior continued, and six days later, they were listening to the radio when an official address came over the airwaves. We went into the mine, but before long the whistle blew, which meant all workers were to report to the yard.

When we came out, one of the meanest foremen stood in front of us with an interpreter.

"We have been ordered by His Holiness the Emperor to inform all prisoners that the Empire of Japan has surrendered to the United States of America. Your occupying forces will be here in a few days. Until then, you are free to come and go as you please. We are to provide you with whatever assistance we are able," the translator announced.

All the men were jumping and hollering and clapping each other on the back. Then they started to filter back toward the camp. A flight of bombers zoomed overhead wiggling their wings back and forth. I looked around for Gunny but couldn't find him in the crowd. How was I supposed to feel? Part of me suspected this was all a trick.

As the rest of the men slowly made their way back to the camp, I trailed behind. I quickly glanced at the office to see the foremen and guards talking animatedly. It looked to me as if they were up to something.

I slipped from the pack of men and crossed toward the pile of rocks where I'd hidden the detonator. But when I snuck to the back of the pile, what I saw made me jump. There sat Gunny.

"Howdy, Tree," he said. "You hear the news?"

"Yeah."

"So what do ya think?"

"I'm not sure. I still feel like a prisoner. I think this could be some kind of trick to throw us off balance."

"Hmm. Them bombers seemed to believe it. I think the war is over, Tree."

I didn't answer. Instead, I lifted the detonator out of its hiding place and fastened the cord to it.

"Tree. Ya can't. Do this thing and yer gonna regret it the rest of your life."

"I doubt that."

"Listen, Tree . . ."

"No! You listen, Gunny! My whole life I've been kicked and beaten. I'm tired, Gunny. Tired of being scared. Tired of always being on the receiving end of whatever the guys in power want to shovel my way. The Japanese have treated us worse than dogs. And now they should reap what they sow."

"Scared? Ya might of been a scared kid once upon a time, Tree. But ya ain't no more. Ya fought like a demon the last four years. Ya stood up to them guards in Camp O'Donnell. Ya rescued me and saved Sergeant Martin. Whatever ya think about yerself is just wrong. Yer the bravest Marine I ever met."

"No, all I've done is take a beating. But I'm done taking it. They have to pay for what they did."

I knew Gunny understood, but that didn't stop him from arguing with me. "These men ain't your enemy no more. The war is over. I know you're feelin' angry. You want revenge. But ya still got a future, kid. And revenge won't fill that hole ya got inside ya right now."

"Gunny, you've been good to me. But I'm done listening to you. I'm doing this."

"No, you ain't. Give me the detonator, Tree. I'm orderin' ya."

"No."

"Ya disobeying a direct order?"

"Yes."

"So I gotta bring you up on charges?"

"I guess so, Gunny."

He looked down at the ground for a while, his arms resting on his elbows. With a deep sigh he looked up at me. There was a look in his eyes I hadn't seen since before the surrender.

"Give me the detonator, Tree."

I looked down at the tiny little instrument in my hand. I was amazed at how such small things could kill so many people. I sighed and handed the detonator to Gunny.

"That's good, son," he said. Then he pushed the plunger on the detonator. The explosion was loud, and the shock wave drove me to my knees. It was good we were behind the rock pile or I might have literally lost my head. I stepped up and peered over. There was nothing left of the office. It was a pile of rubble.

I looked at Gunny. "What? Why did you do it?"

Gunny slowly rose to his feet. "I can carry it. You can't. Before ya got here, them guards carried two heavy machine guns into the office. I reckon they were plannin' to gun us all down before they took off. I won't lose a night's sleep. Because you're right, they oughta answer for their sins. There's evil in the world, Tree. And when you find it, you gotta be the one to stand up and put it down like a rabid dog. And once it's down, ya gotta make sure it don't ever get up again." He put his hand on my shoulder. "What say we figure out a way to get home?"

EPILOGUE

American troops arrived a couple of days after the surrender. The remaining guards and most of the civilians in the area had disappeared. Eventually we were evacuated to a hospital ship, where our wounds were treated and officers debriefed us. But after all of the official stuff was taken care of, we had a lot of time to reflect. The orderlies caught us up on everything that had happened in the world and the war for the last four years. We learned the loud boom we'd heard just days earlier had been the atomic bomb dropping on Nagasaki. It took some time to wrap our minds around it. One month later I was back in Duluth.

When I got to the farm, the house was all closed up. The outbuildings were boarded over, and there was a note on the door from the Millers, who lived down the road. A cab had dropped me off, so I walked over to their place. I'd been fed and medicated on the ship, and had even managed to gain a little weight. I was feeling stronger than I had in ages. It felt good to walk in the cool, brisk air.

Mr. Miller answered the door. Seeing his blond hair, glasses, and weathered face was like a confirmation I was really home and not dreaming. It was around lunchtime, or he would have been out in the fields. Mrs. Miller was a plump, small woman, and her gray hair was pulled up in a bun. She rushed toward me.

"Oh, Henry, you poor, poor boy," she said as she held my face in her hands. She had to stand on her tiptoes to do it.

"I'm okay, Mrs. Miller. Really, I am."

"Nonsense," she said. "I'll bet you haven't had a home-cooked meal in . . ." She stopped and hurried about the kitchen, gathering me a plate of fried chicken, mashed potatoes and gravy, sauerkraut, and a huge slice of chocolate cake for dessert. It was the best meal I'd ever had.

"What happened at our place?" I asked Mr. Miller between bites. "Why is it all closed up? Where's my father and my grandfather?"

Mr. Miller was quiet and looked out the window a minute. Mrs. Miller just looked down at the table.

"I'm afraid your grandfather passed away two years ago," Mr. Miller finally said. "When you'd been missing a while, he told your father what you'd done. Run off and joined the Marines. And it was clear to everyone around that nobody blamed you for leaving. When your pa found out you'd been captured, he just quit. Moved into town and . . ."

"What? It's okay, Mr. Miller, you can tell me."

"I'm sorry, boy. He deeded over your property to me. Now he sits in Spence's all day drinking. He doesn't . . . I'm sorry, lad."

I tried to take it all in. It was a lot to wrap my head around all at once.

"I've been trying to take care of the place best I can, but since Jeb still isn't back from Europe, it got to be too much upkeep for me, so I sold your livestock." He reached over to a small drawer in their kitchen and removed an envelope. "Here is the money. I got a pretty fair price."

He shoved the envelope across the table toward me. I tried to push it back.

"You deserve to be paid for what you did, taking care of things."

"Henry. Son. You are not leaving this house without that money."

I put the envelope in my pocket. "Thank you, sir."

"Your dad, he gave me the farm for far less than its value. I tried to . . . do the right thing. There's more money in there for the rest of what the property is worth.

Unless you want the land back. Just say so and it's yours," he said. "Whatever you want to do is fine with me."

I was quiet a moment. Truth was I didn't know what I wanted to do. After a long moment I said, "I think I'll let you keep it. There's nothing here for me anymore."

"Maybe you should take some time and think about it," Mrs. Miller said.

"No, ma'am. Truth of it is, this place no longer felt like home even before I left."

Once we had everything settled, I went back to the farm and took a few things from the house: a picture of my mother, one of my grandfather, and a few little knick-knacks that reminded me of them. None of my clothes fit me anymore, and there wasn't anything else I wanted. Mr. Miller drove me into Duluth, where I bought a good used truck. On my way out of town, I stopped to get some flowers, then went to the cemetery and said goodbye to Grandpa and visited my mother's grave. I was almost ready to leave Minnesota for good. There was just one thing I had left to do.

I pulled up in front of Spence's, parking on the street. Inside the bar it was dark and smoky. I could hear the clack of billiard balls coming from the back room. There were only a few people around at this time of day. I spotted my father at the end of the bar, a half-empty glass in front of him. His head hung down, and he stared at the bar top as if the answers to all of life's questions were hidden there. He didn't look up as I approached.

"Hello, Pa," I said. At first he didn't respond. "Pa?" I said.

When he finally looked up and swung around, he was so drunk he nearly fell off the barstool. He closed one eye as he tried to focus on my face. Somehow the fact he didn't recognize me at first didn't bother me.

"Wha?" he muttered.

"It's me, Pa. Henry."

He closed both eyes as if he were trying to concentrate. "You!" he said. His eyes flew open, and anger clouded his face. When he tried to stand he stumbled, his feet catching on the barstool legs, and fell to the floor.

I looked down at him. He was pathetic.

"Help me up," he shouted.

I shoved my hands in my pockets. For a brief moment I was ashamed of myself for being afraid of such a weak, wretched man for so long. How had I let him intimidate me? What would my mother think of me? And then I knew. She would be proud of me. Proud of what I had done. Of what I had endured. That was all I needed.

“See you around, Pa,” I said as I turned and walked out.

I never saw him again.

Three days later, I turned onto a dirt driveway that led to a ranch outside Denton, Texas. It was a long drive that divided two pastures that held Black Angus cattle on one side and Longhorns on the other.

I stopped in front of a small, neatly kept ranch house with a shaded front porch running the length of the house. Gunny sat in a wheelchair on the porch. He’d had trouble walking ever since the surrender. The doctors hadn’t quite figured out why yet.

“Yer all the way back to bein’ a tree, I see,” he said as I climbed the porch steps.

“Gunny, you’re a sight for sore eyes.”

“If that’s true, ya ain’t gettin’ out enough.”

We looked at each other a minute. “I was hoping you might have work for me,” I told him. “I need a job.”

“Why would I hire a dumb ex-Devil Dog?”

“Well, for one thing, that’s a pretty mangy herd of Longhorns you got in that pasture. Looks like you need someone around here who knows their way around a cow.”

“I already got a hired man. Besides, I don’t own them Longs to sell for meat. I just like lookin’ at ’em. They remind me of simpler times.”

"Well, Gunny, in case you haven't noticed, you're a little banged—"

"Don't you never shut up? Never did know when to stop talkin'. Of course you got a job. Ten dollars a week, food and found. But there are a couple a conditions."

"I'm listening."

"One: You gotta get a proper hat. That campaign hat yer wearin' has always looked ridiculous on that giant onion of yours."

"Sounds fair."

"Two: You agree to let me introduce ya to my neighbor's daughter, Becky. Pretty as a fresh glass of iced tea and exactly yer age. Take her to a picture show and maybe an ice cream after. Somethin' like that. Those are the terms."

He looked at me. The glint was back in his eye. He might not ever be the rugged, strong oak tree of a man he once was. But in his gaze I saw Gunnery Sergeant Jack McAdams once again.

I put out my hand, and he took it in his. His grip was firm.

"That sounds like a deal."

AFTERWORD

All of the men and women who have served our country in uniform deserve our profound respect. It can be a fruitless exercise to make comparisons between wars in different eras—the battles, combat styles, and horrible conditions fighting men and women face each present their own unique challenges. In conflicts throughout history, captured prisoners have endured unimaginable torture and hardship. In World War II, however, there was a sharp contrast between how prisoners of war were treated in Japanese prison camps and those in Germany.

Statistics show that POWs had an average 4 percent mortality rate in German camps. In the South Pacific, mortality rates for prisoners climbed as high as 30 percent, and in some camps they reached more than 50 percent. These numbers refer to Allied prisoners, whose governments kept records of personnel who did not return home. But in addition to American, Australian, British, and Dutch prisoners, the Japanese captured tens of thousands of Filipino, Korean, and Chinese men and women, and thousands of indigenous peoples in Southeast Asia. The exact number of prisoners who died in Japanese custody will never be known.

The Japanese Empire signed the Geneva Convention, but did not ratify it. They did not consider themselves subject to the "rules of war." In Japan in the 1930s and 1940s, the ancient samurai code of *Bushido* still reigned. And that code said that an enemy who surrendered was considered beneath contempt and owed nothing. Because of this belief, thousands of prisoners were systematically starved, tortured, beaten, or allowed to perish from the multitude of diseases that ran rampant through the camps.

The characters in this book are fictitious. However, all of the incidents of torture and abuse are taken directly from firsthand accounts of prisoners who survived both the Bataan Death March and internment from the surrender of Philippine forces until their liberation at the end of the war. In order to ensure the privacy of those who suffered this specific torture and abuse, I not only changed names, but also many of the unit designations. For example, there was no 15th Marine Infantry Battalion in the Philippines. The 2nd Australian Imperial Force did serve in the Philippines, though the Aussies in the story are fictional. The Australians were tremendous allies to US soldiers in the camps, and I wanted to honor their compassion and bravery toward their American allies by acknowledging them in this way.

Thousands of prisoners were taken to Japan and forced into hard labor to feed the empire's faltering war machine. In many cases, the conditions they faced there were even worse than in internment camps. They worked long shifts seven days a week, and were given minimal food to survive. They were required to meet unreasonable quotas of work each day. When they didn't, they had their rations cut or suffered beatings.

Whereas the prisoners endured heat, humidity, and monsoons in the Philippines, they faced hot summers and freezing winters in Japan. Worker safety was never considered, and men were forced to toil in steel mills and mines without protective gear or safety equipment. Many of the companies they worked for are still profiting from the work of American prisoners during the war years. These corporations have never paid reparations to the prisoners or their families.

What happened in *Prisoner of War* is based on a true story. Numerous underage soldiers and sailors entered the service in World War II. These men and women grew up in an era where record keeping, birth certificates, and proof of identity were not as well documented as they are today. Papers were easy to forge. Birth records were sketchy. Any adult relative could vouch for the age of an enlistee. If the military could accurately determine that an underage member was serving in its ranks, the serviceman was immediately discharged and sent home. However, hundreds if not thousands of Americans entered the service underage and spent their early teenage years fighting fascism, trying to survive combat or, in this case, imprisonment.

When the war ended, Americans rejoiced. But most prisoners returned home long after the celebrations and parades had passed. And in many cases, their own government did not always provide the services they needed to assimilate back into civilian life. Many prisoners who needed lifelong medical treatment after liberation were denied benefits because they could not prove their injuries were combat related. Prisoners who testified against guards and camp commandants in war crimes trials were turned away from hospitals. Some had to fight the Department of Veterans Affairs bureaucracy for years in order to receive the treatment they desperately needed.

There is still ongoing litigation regarding reparations to the families of the men and women who were exploited by Japanese corporations. You can get involved in helping to right this injustice. Write to your congressperson and senator to voice your demand for justice for these American heroes. You can also join the Greatest Generation Foundation to help raise money for veteran care and educational programs that help our communities learn about the sacrifices and contributions the men and women who served in World War II made to ensure the freedoms we enjoy today.

SOURCES

Death March: The Survivors of Bataan, Donald Knox, Harcourt, 1981.

Prisoners of the Japanese: POWs of World War II in the Pacific, Gavan Daws, William Morrow, 1994.

Some Survived: An Eyewitness Account of the Bataan Death March and the Men Who Lived Through It, Manny Lawton, Algonquin Books, 2004.

Tumultuous Decade: Empire, Society, and Diplomacy in 1930s Japan (Japan and Global Society), Masato Kimura and Tosh Minohara, University of Toronto Press, 2013.

Unjust Enrichment: How Japan's Companies Built Postwar Fortunes Using American POWs, Linda Goetz Holmes, Stackpole Books, 2000.

With Only the Will to Live: Accounts of Americans in Japanese Prison Camps, 1941–1945, Robert S. La Forte, Ronald E. Marcello, and Richard Himmel, Roman and Littlefield, 1994.

ACKNOWLEDGMENTS

Writing a book just isn't possible without the contributions of so many people. It's been that way with every book I've ever written. Everyone from agents to editors to family to booksellers to readers plays an important role. *Prisoner of War* is no exception.

First, I thank my editor, Jenne Abramowitz, for pushing me to dig deeper and go further into the characters until I was finally able to breathe life into them. I thank my publicist, Brooke Shearouse, for her hard work and support, and my incredible publisher Scholastic, for which I have enormous respect and admiration. I must also give a special thanks to all the folks at Scholastic Book Fairs who do, well—there's no other way to say it—a magical job of getting books in front of hundreds of thousands of young readers across the country every year.

To my writer buddy mafia, Roland Smith, Susan Elizabeth Phillips, Obert Skye, Brad Sneed, Mary Casanova, and Ard Hoyt who are always there to encourage, pick me up, and talk me down when I'm about to toss the laptop out the window. Thanks guys.

And finally, to my family, which is unmatched in familyness. My wife, Kelly, just takes care of everything. My son and daughters, Mick, Rachel, and Jessica, who patiently smile and nod at my horrible puns and endless schemes. And the newest members of our clan, Dan, George, Frank, and Grace, who make a full life fuller. And I won't forget our two dogs, Willow and Apollo. Despite all the mischief, there is nothing like a pup curled up next to you as you're writing to keep you going.

Lastly, I offer my thanks to the men and women who endured the very definition of horror in the camps of the South Pacific during World War II. To those who were lost and to those who made it home, there are no adequate words to thank you for your sacrifice. But I will try. Thank you. Thank you for standing up to tyranny and oppression. For putting aside your lives, dreams, and aspirations to defend a nation.

Thank you for saving the world.

ABOUT THE AUTHOR

Michael P. Spradlin is a *New York Times* bestselling author. His books include *Into the Killing Seas*, *The Enemy Above*, the Youngest Templar trilogy, the Wrangler Award winner *Off Like the Wind!: The First Ride of the Pony Express*, the Killer Species series, and several other novels and picture books. He holds a black belt in television remote control and is fluent in British, Canadian, Australian, and several other English-based languages. He lives in Lapeer, Michigan.

Visit him online at www.michaelspradlin.com.

YOUNG ADULT
FREEPORT MEMORIAL LIBRARY